Arthur Murphy

The Way to Keep Him

A Comedy in Five Acts. Fourth Edition

Arthur Murphy

The Way to Keep Him
A Comedy in Five Acts. Fourth Edition

ISBN/EAN: 9783744792240

Printed in Europe, USA, Canada, Australia, Japan

Cover: Foto ©Andreas Hilbeck / pixelio.de

More available books at **www.hansebooks.com**

THE

WAY TO KEEP HIM,

A

COMEDY

In FIVE ACTS,

As it is performed at the

THEATRE-ROYAL in DRURY-LANE,

By Mr. MURPHY.

Connubio jungam stabili, propriamque dicabo.

VIRG.

THE FOURTH EDITION.

LONDON:

Printed for P. VAILLANT, facing *Southampton-Street* in the *Strand*. MDCCLXI.

9082 6

(Price 1 s. 6 d.)

PROLOGUE.

Spoken by Mr. HOLLAND.

WHEN *first the haughty critic's dreadful rage,*
    With Gothic *fury over-ran the stage,*
Then PROLOGUES *rose, and strove with varied art*
To gain the soft accesses to the heart ;
Thro' all the tuneful tribe th' infection flew,
And each GREAT GENIUS—*his petition drew,*
In formâ pauperis address'd the pit,
With all the gay antithesis of wit.
Their sacred art poor poets own'd a crime ;
They sigh'd in simile ;—they bow'd in rhyme.
For charity they all were forc'd to beg ;
And ev'ry Prologue was " a wooden leg."
   Next these a hardy manly race appear'd,
Who knew no dulness, and no audience fear'd.
From nature's store each curious tint they drew,
Then boldly held the piece to public view.
" *Lo ! here ! exact proportion ! just design !*
" *The bold relief ! and the unerring line !*
" *Mark in soft union how the colours strike !*
" *This, Sirs, you will—or this you ought to like.*"
They bid defiance to the foes of wit,
" *Scatter'd like ratsbane up and down the pit.*"
   Such Prologues were of yore ;—our bard to-night
Disdains *a false compassion to excite,*
Nor too secure your judgment would oppose ;
He packs no jury,—AND HE DREADS NO FOES.
To govern here no party can expect ;
An audience will preserve its own respect.
   Yet premature, nor grown up to full age
His little group uncensur'd walk'd the stage,
His tablet to enlarge his hand he tries,
And bids his canvas glow with various dyes,
Where sense and folly mix in dubious strife,
Alternate rise, and struggle into life.
Judge if with art the mimic strokes be blend,
If amicably light and shade contend ,
The mental features, if he trace with skill ;
—*See the piece first—then damn it, if you will.*

Dramatis Personæ.

MEN.

LOVEMORE,	Mr. GARRICK.
Sir BASHFUL CONSTANT,	Mr. YATES.
Sir BRILLIANT FASHION,	Mr. PALMER.
WILLIAM, Serv. to LOVEMORE,	Mr. KING.
SIDEBOARD, Serv. to Sir BASH.	Mr. ACKMAN.

WOMEN.

The Widow BELLMOUR,	Mrs. CIBBER.
Mrs. LOVEMORE,	Mrs. YATES.
Lady CONSTANT,	Mrs. DAVIES.
MUSLIN, Maid to Mrs. LOVE-MORE,	Mrs. CLIVE.
MIGNIONET, Maid to Mrs. BELL-MOUR,	Mifs BRADSHAW.
FURNISH, Maid to Lady CON-STANT	Mifs HIPPISLEY.
A black Boy belonging to the Widow.	Mr. HURST.

SCENE, LONDON.

THE WAY TO KEEP HIM.

ACT I. SCENE I.

A Room in LOVEMORE's *House*, WILLIAM
at Cards with a Brother Servant.

WILLIAM.

A PLAGUE on it!—I've turn'd out my
game.—Is forty-feven good?——
SERV. Equal.————

WIL. A plague go with it—tearfe to a queen!—
SERV. Equal.

WIL. I've ruin'd my game, and be hang'd to
me.—I don't believe there's a footman in England
plays with worfe luck than myfelf.——Four aces is
fourteen!

SERV. That's hard;—cruel, by Jupiter!

WIL. Four aces is fourteen—fifteen *(plays.)*

SERV. There's your equality.—

WIL. Very well——fixteen *(plays)*——feventeen
(plays.)

Enter MUSLIN.

MUS. There's a couple of you, indeed!—You're
fo fond of the vices of your betters, that you're
fcarce out of your beds, when you muft pretend to
imitate them and their ways, forfooth.—

WIL. Prithee, be quiet, woman, do.—Eighteen
(plays.)—

MUS. Set you up indeed, Mr. Coxcomb.—

WIL. Nineteen! Clubs *(plays.)*

B   MUS.

Mus. Have done with your foolery, will ye ?—
And fend my Lady word—

Wil. Hold your tongue, Mrs, Muflin, you'll
put us out.—What fhall I play ?—I'll tell you, woman, my mafter and I defire to have nothing to fay
to you or your Lady.———Twenty ; Diamonds !
(*plays.*)

Mus. But I tell you, Mr. Sauce-box, that my
lady defires to know when your mafter came home
lalt night, and how he is this morning ?

Will. Prithee, be quiet.—I and my mafter, are
refolv'd to be teiz'd no more by you.——And fo,
Mrs. Go-between, you may return as you came.—
What the devil fhall I play ?—We'll have nothing to
do with you, I tell you.—

Mus. You'll have nothing to do with us !———
But you fhall have to do with us, or I'll know the
reafon why.—(*Snatches the cards out of his hands.*)

Wil. Death and fury!—This meddling woman
has deftroyed my whole game.—

Mus. Now, Sir, will you be fo obliging as to
fend an anfwer to her queftions, how and when your
rake-helly mafter came home laft night ?——

Wil. I'll tell you what, Mrs. Muflin,———you
and my mafter, will be the death of me at laft ; that's
what you will.——In the name of charity, what do
you both take me for ?—Whatever appearances may
be, I am but of mortal mould.—Nothing fuperna-
tural about me. ———

Mus. Upon my word, Mr. Powder-puff !——

·Wil. I have not indeed!———And fo do you
fee, flefh and blood can't hold it always.—I can't
be for ever a flave to your whims, and your fecond-
hand airs.—

Mus. Second-hand airs!—

Wil. Yes, fecond-hand airs! You take 'em at
your ladies toilets with their caft gowns, and fo you
defcend to us with them.—And then, on the other
hand,

hand, there's my mafter!——Becaufe he chufes to
live upon the principal of his health, and fo run out
his whole ftock as faft as he can, he muft have the
pleafure of my company with him in his devil's dance
to the other world.—Never at home, till three, four,
five, fix, in the morning?—

Mus. Ay, a vile, ungrateful man, to have fo
little regard for a wife that doats upon him.—And
your love for me is all of a piece.——I've no patience with you both.—A couple of falfe, perfidious,
abandoned, profligate—

Wil. Hey, hey,—where's your tongue running?
—My mafter is, as the world goes, a good fort of
a civil kind of a hufband, and I,—heav'n help me,—
a poor fimpleton of an amorous, conftant puppy,
that bears with all the follies of his little tyrant
here.——Come and kifs me, you jade, come and
kifs me.—

Mus. Paws off, Cæfar.——Don't think to make
me your dupe.—I know, when you go with him to
this new lady, this Bath acquaintance: and I know
you're as falfe as my mafter, and give all my dues
to your Mrs. Mignionet there.—

Wil. Hufh, not a word of that.—I'm ruined,
preffed, and fent on board a tender directly, if you
blab that I trufted you with that fecret——But to
charge me with falfehood,——injuftice and ingrati-
tude! My mafter, to be fure, does drink an agreeable difh of tea with the widow.—Has been there
every night this month paft.—How long it will laft,
heav'n knows!—But thither he goes, and I attend
him.——I afk my mafter, Sir, fays I, what time
would you pleafe to want me?——He gives me his
anfwer, and then I ftrut by Mrs. Mignionet, without fo much as tipping her one glance; fhe ftands
watering at the mouth, and A pretty fellow that, fays
fhe.——Ay, ay, gaze on, fays I, gaze on;——
I fee what you would be at:——you'd be glad to

have

have me,————you'd be glad to have me!————
But four grapes, my dear! I'll go home and che-
rifh my own lovely wanton ;——and fo I do, you
know I do.————Then after toying with thee, I
haften back to my mafter; later indeed than he defires, but always too foon for him.————He's loth
to part; he lingers and dangles, and I ftand cool-
ing my heels.————O! to the devil I pitch fuch a
life.————

Mus. Why don't you ftrive to reclaim the vile
man then?

Wil. Softly, not fo faft;—I have my talent to
be fure! yes, yes, I have my talent; fome influence
over my mafter's mind: but can you fuppofe, that
I have power to turn the drift of his inclinations,
and lead him as I pleafe——and to whom?——
to his wife! Pfhaw! Ridiculous,——foolifh, and
abfurd!

Mus. Mighty well, Sir! Can you proceed?

Wil. I tell you a wife is out of date, now-a-
days;—time was—but that's all over—a wife's a
drug now; meer tar-water, with every virtue under
heaven, but no body takes it.——

Mus. Well, I fwear I could flap your impudent
face.————

Wil. Come and kifs me, I fay.————

Mus. A fiddleftick for your kiffts, — while you
encourage your mafter to open rebellion againft the
beft of wives.————

Wil. I tell you it's her own fault; why don't
fhe ftrive to pleafe him, as you do me? Come,
throw your arms about my neck——

Mus. Ay, as I ufed to do, Mr. Brazen!

Wil. Then muft I force you to your own good
—(kiffes her)—Pregnant with delight! Egad if my
mafter was not in the next room—

Mus. Hufh! My lady's bell rings,—how long
has he been up?

WIL.

WIL. He has been up—He has been up—'Sdeath
you've fet me all on fire.——

Mus. There, there,———the bell rings again—
Let me be gone———(*going*,) well, but what muft I
fay? When did he come home?

WIL. At five this morning, rubbed his forehead,
damn'd himfelf for a blockhead, went to bed in a
peevish humour, and is now in tip-top fpirits with
Sir Brilliant Fafhion, in the next room.

Mus. Oh lud! That bell rings again—There,
there let me be gone. (*She kiffes him and exit.*

WIL. There goes high and low life contrafted in
one perfon —'tis well I have not told her the whole
of my mafter's fecrets : fhe'll blab that he vifits this
widow from Bath——But if they enquire, they'll be
told, he does not—The plot lies deeper than they
are aware of, and fo they will only get into a puzzle
—hufh ! — yonder comes my mafter and Sir Brilliant—Let me get out of the way.   [*Exit.*

Enter LOVEMORE *and Sir* BRILLIANT.

LOVE. Ha ! ha !—my dear Sir Brilliant—I muft
both pity and laugh at you——thou art metamor-
phofed into the moft whimfical being!—

Sir BRIL. Nay, prithee, Lovemore, truce with
your raillery—it is for fober advice that I apply to
you—

LOVE. Sober advice !—ha ! ha !—Thou art very
far gone indeed—Sober advice !—There is no fuch
thing as talking ferioufly and foberly to the tribe of
lovers—That eternal abfence of mind that poffeffes
ye all—There is no fociety with you — I was damnable company myfelf when I was one of the pining
herd; but a dofe of matrimony has brought me back
again to myfelf,—has cooled me pretty handfomely,
I affure you ;—ay ! and here comes *repetatur Hauf-
tus.*——

Enter

Enter MUSLIN.

Mus. My lady fends her compliments, and defires to know how you are this morning?

Love. Oh! Lord! my head aches woefully—it's the devil to be teazed in this manner—what did you fay, child?

Mus. My lady fent to know how you do, Sir—

Love. Oh! right!—your lady——give her my compliments, and I am very well, tell her—

Mus. She begs you won't think of going out without feeing her——

Love. There again now!—tell her—tell her what you will—I fhall be glad to fee her—I'll wait on her, —any thing—what you will.

Mus. I fhall let my lady know, Sir.—   [*Exit.*

Love. My dear Sir Brilliant, you fee I am an example before your eyes——Put the widow Bellmour entirely out of your head, and let my Lord Etheridge——

Sir Bril. Pofitively no!—my pride is picqued, and my Lord Etheridge fhall find me a more formidable rival than he is aware of.—

Enter WILLIAM.

Wil. Sir Bafhful Conftant is in his chariot at the upper end of the ftreet, and has fent his fervant to know if your honour is at home——

Lov. By all means——I fhall be glad to fee Sir Bafhful (*Exit William.*) Now here comes another mortifying inftance to deter you from all thoughts of marriage.

Sir Bril. Pfhaw! hang him; he is no inftance for me—a younger brother, who has lived in middling life; comes to an eftate and a title on the death of a confumptive baronet, marries a woman of quality, and carries the primitive ideas of his narrow education

cation

ducation into high life—Hang him!—he is no example for me—I remember him when he had chambers in fig-tree court; faunfered and lounged away his time in temple coffee-houfes; fhy of every body, and running into corners of the room to hold a private conference with his cane, which he applied clofely to his mouth *(Mimicks him.)*

Love. But he is a good deal improved fince that time—

Sir Bril. Po! a meer Hottentot! unacquainted with life,—blufhes every moment, and looks fufpicious, as if he imagined you have fome defign upon him.—

Love. Why, I fancy I can explain that—I have found out a part of his charaƈer lately.—You muft know, there is nothing he dreads fo much as being an objeƈt of ridicule; and fo let the cuftoms and fafhions of the world be ever fo abfurd, he complies, left he fhould be laughed at for being particular.

Sir Bril. And fo, thro' the fear of being ridiculous, he becomes fubftantially fo every moment.

Love. Juft fo—and then to fee him fhrink back as it were from your obfervation, cafting a jealous and fearful eye all round him *(Mimicks him.)*

Sir Bril. Ha! ha!—that's his way—but there is fomething worfe in him——his behaviour to his lady—Ever quarrelling, and infulting her with nonfenfe about the dignity of a hufband, and his fuperior reafon.

Love. Why, there again now; his fear of being ridiculous may be at the bottom of that.——I don't think he hates my lady Conftant—She is a fine woman, and knows the world.—There is fomething myfterious in that part of his conduƈt.

Sir Bril. Myfterious!—not to you—he is ever confulting you—you are in all his fecrets.

Love.

Love. Yes! but I never can find any of them out——and yet there is something working within that he would fain tell me, and yet he is shy, and he hints, and he hesitates, and then he returns again into himself, and ends just where he began.——Hark! I hear his chariot at the door——

Sir Bril. Why do you let him come after you?—— he is a sad troublesome fellow, Lovemore.

Love. Nay, you're too severe——come, he has fits of good-nature.

Sir Bril. His wife has fits of good-nature you mean—how goes on your design there?

Love. Po! Po! I have no design, but I take it you are a formidable man in that quarter.

Sir Bril. Who I? Pshaw! no such thing.

Love. Never deny it to me—I know you have made advances.

Sir Bril. Why faith, I pity my lady Constant, and cannot bear to see her treated as she is.

Love. Well!—that's generous—have a care; I hear him—Sir Brilliant, I admire your amorous charity of all things——ha! ha!——hush! Here he comes.

Enter Sir BASHFUL.

Sir Bash. Mr. Lovemore a good morning to you———Sir Brilliant, your servant, Sir.

Sir Bril. Sir Bashful, I am heartily glad to see you—I hope you left my lady well.

Sir Bash. I can't say, Sir; I am not her physician.

Sir Bril. What a brute! well, Lovemore! I must be gone.

Love. Why in such a hurry?

Sir Bril. I must——I promised to call on a lady over the way—A relation of mine from Wiltshire—I shan't stay long—I shall be with you again before you are dressed.

Love.

Love. Very well!——a l'honneur.

Sir Bril. Sir Bashful, your servant—Mr. Lovemore, yours.   [*Exit.*

LOVEMORE *and Sir* BASHFUL.

Sir Bash. Mr. Lovemore, I am glad he is gone;
for I have something to advise with you about.

Love. Have you?

Sir Bash. I have had another brush with my
wife!

Love. I am sorry for it, Sir Bashful.—I am perfectly glad of it.   [*Aside.*

Sir Bash. Ay! and pretty warm the quarrel was.
" Sir Bashful," says she, " I wonder you will dis-
" grace yourself at this rate——you know my pin-
" money is not sufficient.——My mercer has been
" with me again—I can't bear to be dunn'd at this
" rate ;"—and then she added something about her
quality—you know, Mr. Lovemore, (*smiling*) she is
a woman of quality.

Love. Yes, and a fine woman too!

Sir Bash. no—no—no—do you think she is a
fine woman?

Love. Most certainly!—a very fine woman!—

Sir Bash. (*smiling*) why, yes!——I think she is
what you may call a fine woman.—She keeps good
company Mr. Lovemore.

Love. The very best.

Sir Bash. Yes, yes; that she does; your tip-
top; none else;—but one would not encourage her
too much for all that, Mr. Lovemore—The world
would think me but a weak man, if I did.

Love. Why yes; the world will talk.

Sir Bash. Ay! so it will ;—and so I answered her
stoutly. Madam, says I, a fig for your quality—
don't quality me—I'll act like a man of sense; Madam, and I'll be master in my own house, Madam ;
— I have made a provision for the issue of our mar-

C   riage

riage in the fettlement, Madam; and I would have
you to know, that I am not obliged to pay for your
cats and your dogs, and your fquirrels, and your
monkeys, and your gaming debts.

Love. How could you? that was too ſharply
ſaid—

Sir Bash. I gave it her—but for all that *(ſmiling)* I
—I—I am—very good natured at the bottom, Mr.
Lovemore.

Love. I dare fay you are Sir Baſhful—

Sir Bash. Yes, yes; but a man muſt keep up his
own dignity—'Ill tell you what I did——I went
to the mercer myſelf, and paid him the money
(ſmiles at him.)

Love. Did you?

Sir Bash. I did; but then one would not let the
world know that—no—no—

Love. By no means.—

Sir Bash. It would make them think me too ux-
orious.

Love. So it would!—I muſt encourage that no-
tion of his *(aſide.)*

Sir Bash. And fo I told him; Mr. Luteſtring,
fays I, mum's the word—there is your money, but
let no body know that I paid you ſlily.

Love. Well! you have the handfomeſt way of
doing a genteel thing—

Sir Bash. But that is not all I have to tell you.

Love. No!

Sir Bash. No—no— *(ſmiles)* I have a deeper fecret than that.

Love. Have ye?

Sir Bash. I have;—may I truſt you?

Love. O! upon my honour—

Sir Bash. Well! well! I know you are my friend
——I know you are, and I have great confidence in
you—you muſt know——

Enter

Enter MUSLIN.

Mus. Sir, My lady defires to know if you will drink a difh of tea this morning?

Love. I defire I may not be teazed in this manner—tell your miftrefs—go,—go about your bufinefs.—   [*Turns her out.*

Sir Bash. (*afide.*) Ay! I fee he does not care a cherry-ftone for his wife.

Love. I hate this interruption—Well Sir Bafhful—

Sir Bash. No; he dces not care a pinch of fnuff for her.   [*Afide.*

Love. Proceed Sir Bafhful—

Sir Bash. It does not fignify, Mr. Lovemore; it's a folifh affair; I won't trouble you about it—

Love. Nay; that's unkind—

Sir Bash. Well! well!—I will—I will—But pray do you think Muflin did not over-hear us?

Love. Not a fyllable—come, come, we are fafe.

Sir Bash. I don't know whether I may venture to tell him—[*afide.*] Let me afk you a queftion firft—Pray now, have you any regard for your lady?

Love. The higheft value for her.

Sir Bash. I repofe it with you—You muft know, Mr. Lovemore—as I told you—I—I—I am at the bottom a very good-natured man, and tho' appearances in fome fort—We are interrupted again.—

Enter Sir BRILLIANT.

Sir Bril. Well, I have paid my vifit, Lovemore.

Love. This is the moft crofs accident——fo Sir Brilliant!—

Sir Bash. Ah! I fee there is no going on now—Mr. Lovemore, I wifh you a good day.

Love. Po! Prithee! you fhan't go.—

C 2   Sir

Sir BASH. yes, yes ; another time will do;—suppose you call at my houfe at one ò'clock—no body fhall interrupt us there——   [*Afide to* Lovemore.

LOVE. With all my heart.

Sir BASH. Do fo then ; do fo—we'll be fnug by ourfelves—Well, Mr. Lovemore, a good morning —Sir Brilliant, I kifs your hand—you won't forget, Mr. Lovemore!

LOVE. Depend upon me.

Sir BASH. Very well!——he is the only friend I have.   [*Exit.*

LOVEMORE, *Sir* BRILLIANT.

LOVE. ha! ha!—you broke in upon us in the moft critical moment—He was juft going to communicate——

Sir BRIL. I beg your pardon ; I did not know——

LOVE. Nay, it's no matter ; I fhall get it out of him another time.

Enter MUSLIN.

Mus. My lady, Sir, is quite impatient.

LOVE. Pfhaw! for ever teazing—I'll wait upon her.   [*Exit* Muflin.

Sir BRIL. I'll ftep and entertain her while you drefs—may I take that liberty, Lovemore?

LOVE. You know you may ; no ceremony ; how could you afk fuch a queftion?—apropos ; Sir Brilliant!—Step for one moment into my ftudy—I want juft one word with you——

Sir BRIL. I attend you—

LOVE. This abfurd Sir Bafhful!—ha! ha! a ridiculous, unaccountable—ha! ha!   [*Exeunt.*

SCENE *another Apartment* ; *Mrs.* LOVEMORE *and a Maid attending her.*

Mrs. LOVE. —This trafh of tea!—I don't know why I drink fo much of it.—Heigh ho!—I wonder what keeps Muflin—do you ftep, child, with my com-

compliments to your master, and let him know, I shall be glad of his company to a dish of tea this morning.———

MAID. Yes, Ma'am.——— [*Exit.*

Mrs. LOVE. Surely, never was any poor woman treated with such cruel indifference; nay, with such an open undisguised insolence of gallantry.

Enter MUSLIN.

Mrs. LOVE. Well, Muslin, have you seen his prime minister ?—

Mus. Yes, Ma'am, I have seen Mr. William, and he says, as how my master came home according to custom, at five this morning, and in a huge pickle. —He's now in his study, and has Sir Brilliant Fashion with him.

Mrs. LOVE. Is he there again ?

Mus. He is Ma'am; and I heard them both laughing as loud as any thing.———

Mrs. LOVE. About some precious mischief, I'll be sworn; and all at my cost too !—heigh ho !

Mus. Dear Ma'am, why will you chagrine your-self about a vile man, that is not worth,—no, as I live and breathe,—not worth a single sigh ?———

Mrs. LOVE. What can I do, Muslin ?

Mus. Do, Ma'am! Lard !—If I was as you, I'd do for him ;—As I am a living christian, I would— If I could not cure my grief, I'd find some comforts, that's what I would.

Mrs. LOVE. Heigh ho!—I have no comfort.—

Mus. No comfort, Ma'am ?—Whose fault then ? —Would any body but you, Ma'am ?—It provokes me to think of it.—Would any body, Ma'am, young and handsome as you are, with so many accomplish-ments, Ma'am, sit at home here, as melancholy as a poor servant out of place ?—And all this for what ? —Why for a husband, and such a husband !———

What

What do you think the world will fay of you, Ma'am, if you go on this way?

Mrs. Love. I care not what they fay,—I am tired of the world, and the world may be tired of me, if it will :—My troubles are my own only, and I muſt endeavour to bear them —Who knows what patience may do?——If Mr. Lovemore has any feeling left, my refignation may fome day or other have its effect, and incline him to do me juſtice.

Mus. But, dear Ma'am, that's waiting for dead mens fhoes,—incline him to do you juſtice!—What fignifies expecting and expecting?—Give me a bird in the hand.—Lard, Ma'am, to be for ever pining and grieving!—Dear heart!—If all the women in London, in your cafe, were to fit down and die of the fpleen, what would become of all the public places?——They might turn Vaux-hall to a hop-garden, make a brew-houfe of Ranelagh, and let both the play-houfes to a methodiſt preacher. We fhould not have the racketting with 'em we have now.——" John, let the horfes be put to—
" John, go to my lady Trumpabout's, and invite
" her to a fmall party of twenty or thirty card-
" tables.—John, run to my lady Cat-gut, and let
" her ladyfhip know I'll wait on her to the new
" opera.—John, run as faft as ever you can, with
" my compliments to Mr. Varney, and tell him I
" fhall take it as the greateſt favour on earth, if he
" will let me have a fide-box for the new play.—
" No excufe, tell him."—They whifk about the town and rantipole it with as unconcerned looks, and as florid outfides, as if they were treated at home like fo many goddeffes, tho' every body knows poffef-fion has *ungoddeffed* them all long ago, and their hufbands care no more for them,—no by jingo, no more than they do for their hufbands.—

Mrs. Love. You run on at a ftrange rate.—

Mus. (*In a paſſion.*) Dear Ma'am, 'tis enough to
make

make a body run on—If every body thought like
you———

   Mrs. Love. If every body lov'd like me.—

   Mus. A brass thimble for love, if it is not answered by love.—What the duce is here to do ?—
Shall I go and fix my heart upon a man, that shall
despise me for that very reason, and, " Ay," says
he, " poor fool, I see she loves me,—the woman's
" well enough, only she has one inconvenient cir-
" cumstance about her : I'm married to her, and
" marriage is the devil."——And then, when he's
going a roguing, smiles impudently in your face,
and, " My dear, divert yourself, I'm just going to
" kill half an hour at the chocolate-house, or to peep
" in at the play ; your servant, my dear, your ser-
" vant."—Fye upon 'em !—I know 'em all.—Give
me a husband that will enlarge the circle of my innocent pleasures :———but a husband now-a-days,
Ma'am, is no such a thing.—A husband now—as I
hope for mercy, is nothing at all but a scare-crow,
to shew you the fruit, but touch it if you dare.—A
husband—the devil take 'em all—Lord forgive me
for swearing—is nothing at all but a bug-bear, a
snap-dragon ; a husband, Ma'am, is—

   Mrs. Love. Prithee, peace with your tongue, and
see what keeps that girl.

   Mus. Yes, Ma'am,—why Jenny,—why don't you
come up to my lady ?—What do you stand a gos-
sipping there for ?—A husband, Ma'am, is a mere
monster ;—that is to say, if one makes him so ;
then, for certain, he is a monster indeed ;—and if
one does not make him so, then he behaves like a
monster ; and of the two evils, by my troth———
Ma'am, was you ever at the play of Catharine and
Mercutio ?—The vile man calls his wife his goods,
and his chattles, and his houshold stuff.—There you
may see, Ma'am, what a husband is,—a husband is

                                              —But

—But here comes one will tell you—Here comes Sir Brilliant Fashion.—Ask his advice, Ma'am.

Mrs. Love. His advice! Ask advice of the man who has estranged Mr. Lovemore's affections from me!

Mus. Well, I protest and vow, Ma'am, I think Sir Brilliant a very pretty gentleman.—He's the very pink of the fashion ;—he dresses fashionably, lives fashionably, wins your money fashionably, loses his own fashionably, and does every thing fashionably, and then, he is so lively, and talks so lively, and so much to say, and so never at a loss.—But here he comes.

Enter Sir BRILLIANT *singing.*

Sir Bril. Mrs. Lovemore, your most obedient very humble servant.—But, my dear madam, what always in a vis-a-vis party with your *Suivante !*—You will afford me your pardon, my dear Ma'am, if I avow that this does a little wear the appearance of misanthropy.

Mrs. Love. Far from it, Sir Brilliant—We were engaged in your panegyric.—

Sir Bril. My panegyric !—Then am I come most apropos to give a helping hand towards making it complete.—Mr. Lovemore will kiss your hand presently, Ma'am ;—he has not as yet entirely adjusted his dress.—In the mean time, I can, if you please, help you to some anecdotes, which will perhaps enable you to colour your canvas a little higher.

Mrs. Love. I hope you will be sure, among those anecdotes, not to omit the egregious exploit of seducing Mr. Lovemore entirely from his wife.

[*She makes a sign to* Muslin *to go.*

Sir Bril. I, Ma'am !—Let me perish, Ma'am—

Mrs. Love. Oh ! Sir, I am no stranger to—

Sir Bril. May fortune eternally forsake me, and beauty frown on me, if ever—

Mrs.

Mrs. Love. Don't proteſt too ſtrongly, Sir Brilliant—

Sir Bril. May I never hold four by honours—

Mrs. Love. Nay, but Sir.—

Sir Bril. Ma'am, I am altogether ſtruck with amazement.——May I never taſte the dear delight of breaking a Pharaoh bank, or bullying the whole room at a brag-party, if ever I was, in thought, word, or deed, acceſſary to his infidelity.---I deny all unlawful confederacy. ———

Mrs. Love. O! Sir, it is in vain to deny.

Sir Bril. Nay, but my dear Mrs. Lovemore, give me leave.----I alienate the affections of Mr. Lovemore !----Conſider, Madam, how would this tell in Weſtminſter-hall.----Sir Brilliant Faſhion, How ſay you, guilty of this indictment, or not guilty?----Not guilty, poſs. ---Thus iſſue is joined; ----you enter the court, and in ſober ſadneſs charge the whole plump upon me, without a word as to the how, when, and where ;----No proof poſitive, ----there ends the proſecution.

Mrs. Love. But, Sir, your ſtating of the caſe----

Sir Bril. Dear Ma'am, don't interrupt.----

Mrs. Love. Let me explain this matter.----

Sir Bril. Nay, Mrs. Lovemore, allow me fair play.----I am now upon my defence.----You will pleaſe to conſider, gentlemen of the jury, that Mr. Lovemore is not a ward, nor I a guardian; that he is his own maſter to do as he pleaſes; that Mr. Lovemore is fond of gaiety, pleaſure, and enjoyment; that he knows how to live; to make uſe of the ſenſes nature has given him, and pluck the fruit that grows around him. That is the whole affair.

How ſay ye?----Gentlemen of the jury?----Not guilty.----There, Ma'am, you ſee, Not guilty.

Mrs. Love. You run on finely, Sir Brilliant ;---- but don't imagine that this bantering way----

Sir

Sir Bril. Acquitted by my country, Ma'am you fee,----fairly acquitted!----

Mrs. Love. After the very edyfying counfel you give Mr. Lovemore, this loofe ftrain of yours, Sir Brilliant, is not at all furprifing ;----and, Sir, your late project----

Sir Bril. My, late project !----

Mrs. Love. Yes, Sir : Not content with leading Mr. Lovemore, into a thoufand diffipations from all conjugal affection and domeftic happinefs, you have lately introduced him to your Mrs. Bellmour.-----

Sir Bril. Ma'am, he does not fo much as know Mrs. Bellmour.

Mrs. Love. Fye upon it, Sir Brilliant!---- falfehood is but a poor----

Sir Bril. Falfehood I difdain, Ma'am,----and I Sir Brilliant Fafhion declare, that Mr. Lovemore, your hufband, is not acquainted with the widow Bellmour ;----You don't know that lady, Ma'am. ----But I'll let you into her whole hiftory,----her whole hiftory, Ma'am :----Pray be feated. The widow Bellmour is a lady of fo agreeable a vivacity, that it is no wonder all the pretty fellows are on their knees to her ---Her manner fo entertaining, fuch quicknefs of tranfition from one thing to another ; and every thing fhe does, does fo become her;---- and then fhe has fuch a feeling heart, and fuch generofity of fentiment!-- -

Mrs. Love. Mighty well Sir!----She is a very Veftal----and a Veftal from your fchool of painting muftbe very curious. But give me leave, Sir--- How comes it that you defift from paying your addreffes in that quarter ?

Sir Bril. Why faith, I brib'd her chambermaid, and I find that my lord George Etheridge,—who I thought was out of the kingdom,—is the happy man ; and fo all that remains for me, is to do ju-

llice

ftice to the lady, and confole myfelf in the beft manner I can for the infufficiency of my pretenfions.

Mrs. Love. And am I really to believe all this?

Sir Bril. May the firft woman I put the queftion to, ftrike me to the center with a fupercilious
eyebrow, if every fyllable is not minutely true,----
fo that you fee, Ma'am, I am not the caufe of your
inquietude. ----There is not on earth a man that could
be more averfe from fuch a thing,----nor a perfon
in the world, who more earneftly afpires to prove the
tender efteem he bears ye,----*(She rifes difconcerted.)*
----You fee, my dear Ma'am, we both have caufe of
difcontent ; we are both difappointed,---both croffed
in love,----and fo Ma'am, the leaft we can do is,
both heartily join to----

Lovemore fpeaks within.----William ! Is the Chariot at the door?

Sir Bril. We are interrupted.----

Enter LOVEMORE.

Love. Very well,--- let the chariot be brought
round directly.---How do you do this morning, my
dear? Sir Brilliant, I beg your pardon.----How do
you do my dear?----   *(With an air of cold civility.)*

Mrs. Love. Only a little indifpofed in mind, and
indifpofition of the mind is of no fort of confequence; not worth a cure.----

Love. I beg your pardon, Mrs. Lovemore; Indifpofition of the mind----Sir Brilliant, that is really
a mighty pretty ring you have on your finger.----

Sir Bril. A bauble : Will you look at it ?

Mrs. Love. Though I have but few obligations
to Sir Brilliant, yet I fancy I may afcribe to him the
favour of this vifit, Mr. Lovemore.

Love. *(Looking at the ring.)*----Nay, now pofitively you wrong me; ---I was obliged to you for
your civil enquiries concerning me this morning,

D 2   and

and so on my part, I came to return the compliment before I go abroad.—Upon my word 'tis very prettily set----*(Gives it.)*

Mrs. Love. Are you going abroad Sir?----

Love. A matter of business;----I hate business ----but business must be done.----*(Examining his ruffles.)*----Pray is there any news?----any news, my dear?

Mrs. Love. It would be news to me, Sir, if you would be kind enough to let me know whether I may expect the favour of your company to dinner.

Love. It would be impertinent in me to answer such a question, because I can give no direct positive answer to it;—as things happen—perhaps I may, —perhaps may not.----But don't let me be of any inconvenience to you;----it is not material where a body eats.----Apropos, you have heard what happened, *(to Sir Brilliant.)*

Sir Bril. When, and where?

Love. A word in your ear——Ma'am with your permission.——

Mrs. Love. That cold, contemptuous civility, Mr. Lovemore——

Love. Pshaw!----Prithee now,----How can you, my dear?----That's very peevish now, and ill-natured.---- It is but about a meer trifle—Hark ye, *(whispers)* I lost every thing I play'd for after you went,----the Foreigner, and he understand one another.——I beg pardon, Ma'am, it was only about an affair at the opera.

Mrs. Love. The opera, Mr. Lovemore, or any thing, is more agreeable than my company.

Love. You wrong me now, I declare you wrong me;----and if it will give you any pleasure, I'll sup at home.----Can't we meet at the St. Alban's to-night? ----*(aside to Sir Brilliant.)*

Mrs. Love. I believe I need not tell you what
pleasure

pleafure that would give me : But unlefs the pleafure is mutual, Mr. Lovemore.——

Lovl. Ma'am I----I----I perceive all the delicacy of that fentiment ;-----But----a----I fhall in-
comode you,-----you poffibly may have fome private party---and it would be very unpolite in me, to
obftruct your fchemes of pleafure.----Would it not,
Sir Brilliant? *(laughs.)*

Sir Bril. It would be gothic to the laft degree.
Ha! ha!

Love. Ha! ha!----To be fure, for me to be of
the party, would look as if we lived together like
our friend Sir Bafhful Conftant and his lady, who
are for ever like two game-cocks, ready armed to
goad and wound one another moft heartily.-----Ha!
ha!

Sir Bril. The very thing.----Ha! ha!

Love. So it is,----fo it is. *(Both ftand laughing.)*

Mrs. Love. Very well, gentlemen; you have it
all to yourfelves.

Love. Odfo! *(looking at his watch,)* I fhall be
beyond my time.----Any commands into the city,
Madam?----

Mrs. Love. Commands!----I have no commands,
Sir.

Love. I have an appointment there at my Banker's ;----Sir Brilliant, you know old Difcount?----

Sir Bril. What, he that was in parliament?----

Love. The fame;----Entire Butt, I think, was
the name of the borough.----Ha! ha! ha!----
Can I fet you down any where, Sir Brilliant?

Sir Bril. Can you give me a caft in St. James's
ftreet?

Love. By all means—*Allons*—Mrs. Lovemore,
your moft obedient, M 'am—Who waits there?—
Mrs. Lovemore, no ceremony—your fervant.

(Exit finging.)

Sir

Sir Bril. Ma'am you fee I don't carry Mr. Lovemore abroad now—I have the honour, Ma'am, to take my leave—I fhall have her I fee plainly;—Sir Brilliant mind your hits, and your bufinefs is done. (*Afide.*) Ma'am, your moft obedient.---

(*Exit.*

Enter MUSLIN *haftily.*

Mus. Did you call Ma'am?

Mrs. Love. To be infulted thus by his loofe confident carriage!—

Mus. As I live and breathe, Ma'am, if I was as you, I would not flutter myfelf about it.—

Mrs. Love. About what?

Mus. La! what fignifies mincing matters?—I overheard it all.

Mrs. Love. You did;—did you? (*angrily.*)

Mus. Ma'am!—

Mrs. Love. It does not fignify at prefent.——

Mus, No Ma'am, it does not fignify, and revenge is fweet, I think; and by my troth, I don't fee why you fhould ftand on ceremony with a hufband that ftands upon none with you.

Mrs. Love. Again — prithee, Mrs. Malapert, none of your advice.—How dare you talk in this manner to me?—Let me hear no more of this impertinent freedom.—(*walks about.*)

Mus, No, Ma'am.—It's very well, Ma'am.—I have done, Ma'am, — (*difconcerted, and then fhe fpeaks afide.*)—What the devil is here to do?—An unmannerly thing to go for to huff me in this manner!—

Mrs. Love. (*Still walking about.*) To make his character public, and render him the fubject of every tea-table throughout this town, would only ferve to widen the breach, and, inftead of his negleft, might call forth his anger, and fettle at laft into a fixed averfion --lawyers, parting, and feparate maintenance

would

would enfue.—No,—I muft avoid that,—if poffible;
I will avoid that.—What muft be done?

Mus. What can fhe be thinking of now?—The
fulky thing, not to be more familiar with fuch a
friend as I am!—What can fhe mean?—Did you
fpeak to me Ma'am?———

Mrs. Love. Suppofe I were to try that!—Muflin.

Mus. Ma'am!—Now for it.—

Mrs. Love. You heard Sir Brilliant deny that
Mr. Lovemore vifits at this widow Bellmour's.

Mus. Lard, Ma'am, he is as full of fibs as a
French milliner,—he does vifit there,—I know it
all from William,—I'll be hang'd in my own gar-
ters if he does not.

Mrs. Love. I know not what to do!—Heigh-ho!
—I think I'll venture.—Let my chair be got ready
inftantly.

Mus. Your chair, Ma'am!—Are you going out,
Ma'am?

Mrs. Love. Don't teaze me with your talk, but
do as I bid you,—and bring my capuchin down to
the parlour immediately.   (*Exit.*)

Mus. What is in the wind now?—An ill-natured
pufs, not to tell me what fhe is about.—It's no matter,—fhe does not know what fhe is about—Before
I'd lead fuch a life, I'd take a lover's leap into Ro-
famond's pond.—I love to fee company for my part.
—But, Lord blefs me! I had like to have forgot,—
Mrs. Marmalet comes to my rout to-night.—I had
as live fhe had ftaid away,—She's nothing but mere
lumber!—fo formal, that fhe won't play above a
fhilling-whift.—How the devil does fhe think I'm to
make a fhilling party for her?—There's no fuch a
thing to be done now-a-days,—no body plays fhilling-whift now.

[*Exit in a paffion.*

End of the Firft Act.

A C T   II.

SCENE, a Room at Sir BASHFUL CONSTANT's.

Enter Sir BASHFUL.

DID not I hear a knock at the door ?—yes, yes ;
—I did—the coach is juſt driving away—Sideboard !—Sideboard ! come hither I tell you—come
hither, Sideboard—I muſt know who it is—my wife
keeps the beſt company in England—but I muſt be
wary ; I muſt be cautious ; ſervants love to peep
into the bottom of their maſter's ſecrets.

Enter SIDEBOARD.

Whoſe coach was that at the door but now ?

SIDE. The dutcheſs of Hurricane, pleaſe your
Honour.

Sir BASH. The dutcheſs of Hurricane !—a woman
of great rank *(aſide and laughing.)* The dutcheſs of
Hurricane, Sideboard ! What did ſhe want ?

SIDE. I can't ſay, your Honour——She left this
card.

Sir BASH. A card ! let me ſee it *(reads)* " *The*
" *dutcheſs of* Hurricane's *compliments to lady* Con-
" ſtant ; *ſhe has left the Rooks, and the country Squires,*
" *and the Crows, and the Fox-hunters, and the Dogs,*
" *to their own dear ſociety for the reſt of the winter,*
" *and lets her ladyſhip know that ſhe ſees company at*
" Hurricane-*houſe on* Wedneſdays *for the remainder*
" *of the ſeaſon.*"—Make me thankful ! here's a card
from a dutcheſs !—what have you in your hand ?—

SIDE. Cards they have been leaving here all the
morning, your Honour,

Sir

Sir Bash. All the morning!—why, I may as well keep an inn; may as well keep the coach and horses in Piccadilly—I won't bear this, Sideboard —I can't bear it; it is too much pleasure, (*aside.*) —Let me see;—let me see——

Side. There, your honour——(*Gives him several slips of cards.*)

Sir Bash. (*reads.*) " Lady *Riot*—Mrs. *Almight* " —The dutchefs of *Carmine*——Look ye there! " another dutchefs! Mrs. *Loveit*—Lady *Baffet*—— " Lord *Pleurifie*—The countefs of *Ratifie*——Sir " *Richard Langs* —— Lord *Laudanum* —— Sir " *Charles Valerian*—Lady *Hectic*——Lady *Mary* " *Gabble.*"—What, all thefe this morning, Sideboard? This is too much—all people of tip-top condition to vifit my wife——

Enter FURNISH.

Sir Bash. What's the matter, Furnifh?

Fur. Nothing, Sir; nothing's the matter—

Sir Bash. What are you about?—where are you going? what have you to do now?

Fur. To do fo, Sir!—only to tell the chairmen they muft go out with the chair in the evening, and black George with the flambeau before 'em to pay fome vifits for my lady this evening, that's all, Sir.

Sir Bash. An empty chair to return vifits!—— What polite ways people of fashion have of being intimate with one another!—I can't help laughing at it; I like to fee my wife do like other people— *(laughs afide)* but I fhall be found out by my fervants—I tell you, Sideboard, and I tell you too, Mrs. Impertinence, that my lady leads a life of folly, and noife, and hurry, and cards, and dice, and abfurdity, and nonfenfe, and I won't bear it; I am refolv'd I will not.—I think I hear her coming;—I do; I do;—I will not go on this way, and now I'll tell her roundly a piece of my mind.

E   *Enter*

Enter Lady CONSTANT.

Sir Bash. *(aside.)* She looks charmingly—so, my lady Conftant, I have have had my houfe full of duns again to-day.

Lady Con. obliging creatures! to call fo often— What did they want?

Sir Bash. What did they want? they wanted their money——

Lady Con. Well! and you paid them, did not ye?——

Sir Bash. I pay them!—'sdeath! Madam, what do you take me for?——

Lady Con. I took you for a hufband, but I find I was miftaken——

Sir Bash. Death and fire!—I fee you are an un-grateful woman.—I am fure, my lady Conftant, I have behaved in many inftances with great good-nature towards you. Did not I go into parliament, Madam, to pleafe you? Did not I go and get drunk at a borough for a month together! and get mobbed at the George and Vultur, and pelted and horfe-whipped the day before the election; and all this to pleafe your vanity?—Did not I ftand up in the houfe to make a fpeech merely to gratify your pride? And did not I expofe myfelf there? Did I know whether I ftood upon my head or my heels? What the devil had I to do in parliament?—What's my coun-try to me?——

Lady Con. Who mentioned your country, Sir?

Sir Bash. I defire you won't mention it—I have nothing to do with it,—no, nor with your debts— I have nothing to do with them, and I defire you will tell your people to come no more after me——I know how to put a ftop to that matter—notice in the Gazette will exempt me from your extravagan-cies—I did not live in the Temple for nothing.

Fur.

Fur. I proteſt I never heard any body talk ſo mean in all my days before ——

Lady Con. Don't you be ſo pert, pray? Leave the room; go both of ye down ſtairs.——

[*Exeunt* Furniſh *and* Sideboard.

Sir Bash. I have kept it up pretty well before my ſervants—She is a fine woman, and talks admirably—— (*Aſide.*)

Lady Con. Is there never to be an end of this uſage, Sir Baſhful?—am I to be for ever made unhappy by your humours?

Sir Bash. Humours!—I like that expreſſion prodigiouſly—Humours!—and ſo I ſuppoſe all good ſenſe and ſound judgment are, in the fine lady's dictionary, to be called humours.—Humours indeed!——

Lady Con. You may harp upon the word, Sir—but let me tell you, that ſelf-love is more apt to give falſe colourings to the infirmities it finds in our own breaſt, than the reſt of the world is to miſinterpret our good qualities. Humours you have, Sir, and ſuch as are to me grown inſupportable.——

Sir Bash. She talks like an angel!—Madam, I ſhould have no humours (*moderating his voice*) as you call them, if your extravagancies were not inſupportable.—But let us canvaſs this matter quietly and cooly—What would the world think of my underſtanding, if I were ſeen to encourage your way of life?——

Lady Con. What will the world think of it now, Sir!—Take this along with you, there is a certain ſet of people, who, when they would avoid one error, are ſure to run into the oppoſite extreme.

Sir Bash. There's for you!——a tranſlation from Horace—*Dum vitant ſtulti vitia*—oh! ſhe is a notable woman. (*Aſide.*)

Lady Con. Let me tell you, Sir Baſhful, there is not in the world a more ridiculous ſight than a

perſon

perfon wrapping himfelf up in imaginary wifdom, if he can but guard againft one giant-vice, while he becomes a prey to a thoufand other abfurdities.

Sir Bash. Lord! I am nothing at all to her in an argument. She has a tongue that can reafon me out of my fenfes. I could almoft find it in my heart to tell her the whole truth.——Look'e, Madam, you know—you know my lady Conftant, (*looking gently at her*) that I am—very good-natur'd at the bottom,—and,——and,—any thing in my power,— any thing in reafon————

Lady Con. When did I defire any thing elfe ?— Is it unreafonable to live with decency ?—Is it un-reafonable to keep the company I have been always us'd to ? —Is it unreafonable to conform to the modes of life, when our fortune çan fo well afford it ?—

Sir Bash. She is a very reafonable woman, and I wifh I had but half her fenfe. (*Afide.*) I'll tell you what, my lady Conftant, to avoid eternal difputes, if a fum of money within a moderate compafs—if a brace of hundreds—why fhould not I give her three hundred ?---I did not care if I went as far as three hundred—If three hundred pounds, my lady Con-ftant, will fettle the matter (*in a gentle tone of voice*) why as to the matter of three hundred pounds, I fhould not value much if I————

Enter FURNISH, *with a band-box.*

Fur. Your Ladyfhip's things are fent home from the Milliner's——

Sir Bash. Zookers! this woman has overheard me—As to the matter of three hundred pounds, Madam (*loud and in a paffion*) let me tell you it is a very large fum—Afk me for three hundred pounds, Madam I—Do you take me for a blockhead, to fhovel money away in that manner ?—

Lady Con. What does the man fly out fo for ?—

Sir

Sir Bash. What right have you to three hundred pounds?—I will allow no fuch doings?—Is not my houfe an eternal fcene of your routs, and your drums, and your what-do-ye-call'ems?———— Don't I often come home, when my hall is barricaded with powder-monkey fervants, that I can hardly get within my own doors?

Lady Con. Why all this paffion, Sir?

Sir Bash. Have not I feen you at a game at Loo put the fee fimple of a fcore of my beft acres upon a fingle card?—And have not I muttered to myfelf, if that woman now was as much in love with me, as fhe is with Pam, what an excellent wife would fhe make!

Lady Con. Yes, I have great reafon to love you truly————

Sir Bash. Death and fire! you are fo fond of play, that I fhould not wonder to fee my next child refemble one of the coat-cards, or marked on the forehead with a pair-royal of aces?

Fur. I am fure you deferve to be marked on the forehead with a pair of————

Sir Bash. Get out of the room, you jade; get out of the room. (Exit Furnifh.)

Lady Con. I tell you once for all, Sir, I am quite tired out with your ways—your unaccountable temper is for ever breaking out in fudden onfets of paffion;——Avarice, narrownefs of mind, unprovok'd fallies of ill-humour, want of fpirit to live fuitably to your fortune, thefe are things that I cannot any longer endure;—I am tir'd of blufhing for you, Sir.—

Sir Bash. I have gone too far—She is afham'd of me—

Lady Con. I have often propofed to part, and I muft now infift upon it.

Sir Bash. I would not have it come to that—My lady Conftant, extremities are bad—I am not againft
fpending

ſpending money *(in a ſoftened tone.)* I am only a-
gainſt throwing it away with extravagance—You
know very well, Madam———Oh! ſhe knows but
every thing———I ſay, Madam, you know that if
I could be ſure not to be thought ridiculous———

Lady Con. Ridiculous!—It is worſe than ridiculous, Sir.—The other day, you agreed to a ſeparation ; the articles are ready, and I muſt have
them carried into execution.

Sir Bash. You will have the worſt of that bargain, I fancy ; a ſeparate maintenance will go but a
little way to anſwer the bawling of Milliners, Mer-
cers, Jewellers, and gaming debts.———

Lady Con. It will ſerve at leaſt to purchaſe content, and nothing can procure that under one roof
with you.———

Sir Bash. I have certainly gone too far;—Madam,
if I adviſe you againſt a ſeparation it is for your own
good—you complain of my being haſty, and are more
precipitate yourſelf—We might explain *(looking
tenderly.)* We might explain matters, ſo as to come
to a right underſtanding—but ſo it happens.—I believe you don't know me—If you but knew—S'death
I am going to blab.—I ſay, Madam, if you under-
ſtood—I wiſh ſhe did, and that it was all over.—
And as to the power of a huſband, I want no ty-
rannical uſe of it—I don't know but I might be
brought to give it up—in part at leaſt—and to
connive—Damn it, I am interrupted again.—

Enter FURNISH.

Fur. A ſervant from Mrs. Lovemore, Madam,
wants to know———

Sir Bash. As to the controul of a huſband *(loud and
in a paſſion)* I will never give it up—I will be maſter
in my own houſe, Madam;—and my ſubſtance
ſhall not be ſquandered away as you pleaſe.—

Lady Con. A ſtorm, a whirl-wind is fitter to
converſe with.—   Sir

Sir BASH. I will ſtorm like a whirl-wind in my own houſe—And I tell you once for all, you are an ungovernable woman; your imagination is as wild as any woman's in Bedlam;—and Bedlam is the fitteſt place for you—Do, go thither, go; for I tell you once for all, I will have no more of your doings in my houſe. *(Exit.)*

Lady CONSTANT *and* FURNISH.

Lady CON. His head is certainly turn'd—Did any body ever ſee ſuch behaviour?

FUR. See it! No, nor bear it neither—Your ladyſhip will never be happy, I am afraid, till you part from him.——

Lady CON. Oh! Never—It is impoſſible—He not only has loſt all decency, but has bid adieu to all humanity. That it ſhould be my fate to be married to ſuch a quickſand!—But I'll think no more of him—What did Mrs. Lovemore's ſervant want?

FUR. To know if your Ladyſhip will be at home this morning?—

Lady CON. Yes, I ſhall be at home—Step with me to my room, and I'll write a card to ſend to Mrs. Lovemore—Of all things let a woman beware how ſhe marries a narrow-minded under-bred huſband. *(Exeunt.)*

Enter Sir BASHFUL *and* LOVEMORE.

Sir BASH. Walk in, Mr. Lovemore—walk in— I am heartily glad to ſee you—this is kind.——

LOVE. I am ready, you ſee, to attend the call of friendſhip.—

Sir BASH. Mr. Lovemore, you are a friend indeed.—

LOVE. You do me honour, Sir Baſhful;—pray how does my lady?—

Sir BASH. Perfectly well! never ſaw her look
better---

better—But we have had t'other skirmish since I saw you.—

Love. Another!—

Sir Bash. Ay! another;—and I did not 'bate her an ace—but I told you I had something for your private ear—Pray now have you remarked any thing odd or singular in me?

Love. Not the least—I never knew a man of less oddity in my life.

Sir Bash. What, nothing at all?—He! he!—(*Smiles at him.*) Have you remarked nothing about my wife?

Love. You don't live happy with her;—But that's not singular.

Sir Bash. Po! I tell you, Mr. Lovemore, I am at the bottom a very odd fellow—

Love. Not at all.—

Sir Bash. Yes, yes, yes; I am; am. I indeed; as odd a fish as lives; and you must have seen it before now.—

Love. Not I, truly—You are not jealous, I hope.—

Sir Bash. You have not hit the right nail o'the head—No, no ;—not jealous ;—do her justice, I am secure there ; my lady has high notions of honour; —no, it is not that.—

Love. What then?

Sir Bash. Can't you guess?—

Love. Not I, upon my soul;—explain.

Sir Bash. Mr. Lovemore, I have great dependence upon you—first let me shut this door.

[*Shuts the door.*

Love. In the name of wonder, what whim has got possession of him now?

Sir Bash. You never could have imagined it— I blush at the very thoughts of it—(*Turns away.*)

Love. What's the matter, Sir Bashful?—Come,

1   come,

ith it at once—let me be of yc

Of my council—the very thin
r. Lovemore, the affair is tl
ould betray me!—I shall nev
ace again.———

hats the matter, Sir Bashfu
like a friend ?

Mr. Lovemore, I doubt you
Some men there are, who wh
:e reposed in them, take occa
d a hank over their friend, a
:he rest of his days.

i! fy! this is ungenerous; tr
ither quality; it feells from i
:d by honour.

Mr. Lovemore, I have n
i—Hush!—did not you hea
—there's a shadow under tl
—fervants have a trick of l
hat has he got in his head ?—

(peeping out.) No, no;—i
.ovemore, I will make you
ithful depofitary of a secret
e bottom of my heart, to the i
i——there let it lie conceal'd f
—my inclinations;——Nay,
——

o, upon my honour.—

Well! well! my inclina
ot chang'd——but they are not
ed to be—-I—-I am in lov
oks filly.)

ell! love is a paffion of a
on't tell me any more about
it will find it out, and lay
·I muft not appear an encc

F

this business---No, no---you must not involve me in a quarrel with her.---

.Sir Bash. Po! you don't take me right ;---quite wide of the mark ; hear me out.

Love. I won't indeed ; I won't.

Sir Bash, Nay, nay, but you shall ; you shall.

Love. Positively no ;---let me keep clear ;---- She shall certainly know it, and the devil's in the dice if she does not comply with my desires from a ' meer spirit of revenge. . (*Aside.*)

Sir Bash. I tell you, Mr. Lovemore, the object of my passion—this charming woman, whom I doat on to distraction---

Love. I don't desire to know it.---

Sir. Bash. You must ; you must ; this adore-able creature---

Love. Keep it to yourself, Sir Bashful---

Sir Bash. Is my own wife.---

Love. (*stares at him.*) Your own wife !

Sir. Bash. (*looks silly, blushes, and turns away.*) Yes ; my own wife.---

Love. This is the most unexpected discovery.---

Sir Bash. Look'e there now !---He laughs at me already.

Love. And can this be possible ?---Are you real-ly in love with my lady Constant, your own wife ?

Sir Bash. Spare my confusion, Mr. Lovemore, spare my confusion---ay ! it's all over with me.---

Love. I should never have guessed this, Sir Bash-ful.

Sir Bash. I have made myself very ridiculous, Mr. Lovemore.

Love. Ridiculous !---far from it---why do you think it ridiculous to love a valuable woman ?--- Po ! Po ! clear up man ; and now, to keep you in countenance, I will deposit a secret with you ;--- I love my wife.

Sir Bash. What ?

Love. I am in love with my wife.---

Sir

Sir BASH. Hey!-----(*Looks at him in great glee*) He! he!---No, no---you don't love her;---He! he!---do you?---Do you, Mr. Lovemore?

LOVE. Moſt ardently.

Sir BASH. Give me your hand; give me your hand;—He! he!—I am glad to know this—What, and have you led the life you have done all this time on purpoſe to conceal your love?

LOVE. For that very purpoſe.—I love her moſt ſincerely; but then I would not let her know it for the world.

Sir BASH. Perfectly right; perfectly right.

LOVE. When a woman once finds that a man is weak enough to betray a paſſion for her, ſhe cries VICTORIA directly, falls to plundering, and pre-prepares chains to enſlave the poor devil all the reſt of his life.

Sir BASH. It's the way with them all ſure enough.

LOVE. And the world, Sir Baſhfull, the world is much given to ſcoffing. Do you know, if people were to ſurmiſe any thing of our weakneſs, we ſhould have nothing but wit, and raillery, and fleers, and taunts flying about our ears.

Sir BASH. That's what I have been always afraid of; and ſo I have been conſtantly quarrelling with my lady on purpoſe to cloak the affair, and prevent all ſuſpicion.

LOVE. And it was wiſely done; —— beſides there is another convenience, Sir Baſhful; ———my lady you know has ſome youthful vigour about her, and you are rather a little advanced or ſo.———

Sir BASH. Pſhaw!—it is not for that; that's no-thing; I wear admirably well, Mr. Lovemore!

LOVE. Do you?

Sir BASH. As young as ever!——But I don't let her know that.

LOVE. Ha! ha!---that's right.---Keep to that---Ha! ha!---

Sir

Sir Bash. Yes, yes;----Ha! ha!---I fight cunning, Mr. Lovemore---but then I am main deep in love for all that, and have done her a thoufand kindnefses in the mean time.

Love. Have ye?

Sir Bash. Oh! a multitude---but then it was always in a fly way; cautious and circumfpect!-----I'll tell you now;---She has been plaguing me a long time for a diamond crofs, and diamond buckles ----Madam, fays, I, I'll have no fuch trumpery----but then goes I and befpeaks them of the beft jeweller in town ---all under the rofe tho'!----the buckles are ready---will come to three hundred----She'll have them to-day without knowing where they come from. They'll fet her off to great advantage, Mr. Lovemore. (Smiles.)

Love. So they will.

Sir Bash. And then, I can take occafion to be as jealous as Bedlam when I fee her wear them.

Love. So you can---I wifh he may never be jealous of me in earnefts.-(Afide.)

Sir Bash. Well! give me your hand, my dear brother fufferer. I'll tell you, Mr. Lovemore----we can in a fnug way be of great fervice to each other, if you will come into my fcheme.

Love. As how pray?

Sir Bash. Look'e;---there are fome things, you know, our wives expect to be done.---

Love. So there are.---what is he at now? (Afide.)

Sir Bash. Now if you will affift me---

Love. You may depend upon my affiftance.

Sir Bash. Thus it is then. My lady Conftant wants money---you know fhe keeps a great deal of company, and makes a great figure there;----I wifh fhe could fay the fame of me---

Love. Why truly I wifh fhe could---

Sir Bash. But that's out of the queftion----now I would have you take the money from me,

and

and pretend to lend it to her out of friendship and regard.

Love. Why, you are a very Machiavel!——nothing was ever better conceived——Here's a fellow pimping for his own horns. (*Aside.*)

Sir Bash. Here, here, here ;—take it—here it is in bank notes,—one,—two—three,——there's three hundred ;—give her that,——and tell her you have more at her service to-morrow, or next day, if her occasions require it.

Love. Sir Bashful, I'll do it——this is the rarest adventure! (*Aside.*)

Sir Bash. I'll do any thing for you in return.

Love. I shall have occasion for your friendship— that is to forgive me if you find me out. (*Aside.*)

Sir Bash. You shall always command me—but lose no time; step to her now ; she talked of parting ; step to her and make her easy.

Love. I'll do my endeavour; you may rely upon me ; I'll make her easy if possible.

Sir Bash. That's kind ; that's kind ;—well! Mr. Lovemore, ha! ha!—this is the rarest scheme—is it not ?—ha! ha!——

Love. ha! ha !—it is the newest way of making a wife easy.

Sir Bash. Ay! let this head of mine alone—

Love. That I won't if I can help it (*Aside.*)—— Well!—I'll step to my lady——

Sir Bash. Do so ; do so——

Love. I will ; your servant—who can blame me now if I cuckold this fellow ?—it's all his own seeking——So ridiculous an adventure sure never was (*Aside*)—Your servant Sir Bashful, your servant.——
(*Exit.*)

Sir Bash. Prosper you, prosper you, Mr. Lovemore!—make me thankful !—he is a true friend—this is finely contrived !—Hush !——did not I hear some body coming ?—is not that Sir Brilliant's voice ?—

4   301322   sure

fure they won't let him in—Zookers! he is coming
up ſtairs——He ſhan't ſee my lady for all that——
He ſhan't interrupt buſineſs.

Enter Sir BRILLIANT.

Sir BRIL. Sir Baſhful, I kiſs your hand—and my
lady,—how does ſhe do?—is ſhe at home?———

Sir BASH. Do you think I have nothing to do but
to know whether ſhe is at home or not?——I don't
trouble my head about her, Sir.———

Sir BRIL. Never talk ſo ſlightingly of ſo agreeable a woman. My lady Conſtant has ſpirit, taſte,
ſenſe, wit, beauty.

Sir BASH. Spirit, taſte, ſenſe, wit, beauty—She
has all that ſure enough, *(Aſide.)* Sir, I am no ſworn
appraiſer, to take an inventory of her effects——I
don't know what ſhe has.

Sir BRIL. Is her ladyſhip viſible this morning?

Sir BASH. No, Sir; ſhe is inviſible this morning;
and unintelligible this morning, and incomprehen-
ſible this morning.——She is not well; ſhe has the
vapours; ſhe is not to be ſpoke to.

Sir BRIL. I am ſorry for it—I came to tell her the
rareſt piece of news—Such a diſcovery!

Sir BASH. Ay! what's that?

Sir BRIL. You know Sir Amorous La Fool?

Sir BASH. Mighty well.

Sir BRIL. Poor devil! he has got into ſuch a
ſcrape!

Sir BASH. What's the matter? loſt his money at
play?

Sir BRIL. Worſe! much worſe!

Sir BASH. He is not dead?

Sir BRIL. Why that's a ſcrape indeed!—but it is
not that;

Sir BASH. What then?

Sir BRIL. He is fallen in love—ha! ha!

Sir BASH. With ſome jilt, perhaps?

Sir

Sir Bril. No————

Sir Bash. With fome prude, may be?

Sir Bril. Nor that.

Sir Bash. A young actrefs, or an opera finger?

Sir Bril. No; you'll never guefs—like a filly devil, he has fallen in love with his own wife?

Sir Bash. In love with his own wife! *(Stares at him.)*

Sir Bril. Ha! ha!—it's very true; I heard it at my lady Betty Scandal's; and there was fo much laughing about it; the card-tables were all in afto. nifhment; Whift ftood ftill; Quadrille laid down the cards; and Brag was in fufpenfe—Poor Sir Amorous!—ha! ha!—it is fo very ridiculous—is it not Sir Bafhful?

Sir Bash. *(difconcerted.)* Very ridiculous, indeed! —zoons! its my own cafe directly. *(Afide.)*

Sir Bril. The man is loft, abandoned, ruined, dead, and buried; ha! ha!—you don't laugh Sir Bafhful—

Sir Bash. Who I?—I—I—I—I laugh as heartily as I poffibly can.

Sir Bril. I want to find Lovemore; he will be fo diverted with it—you know he does not care a pinch of fnuff for his wife.

Sir Bash. No more he does—to be fure he does not—ha! ha! *(Afide.)* No; he cares no more for his wife than I do for mine.

Sir Bril. Much the fame.

Sir Bash. Ay! much the fame—he knows but little of us. *(Afide.)*

Sir Bril. Poor Sir Amorous!—he'll! never be able to fhew his face again; adieu for him the fide-box whifper, the foft affignation, and all the joys of freedom—He is retired with his Penelope to love moft heartily for a month, grow indifferent in two, and hate moft heartily in three————

Sir Bash. Do you think it will end fo?

Sir

Sir Bril. Moſt certainly!—but I have not told
you the worſt of his caſe—our friend Sir Charles
Wildfire, you know, was about a comedy—now
what has he done but drawn the character of Sir
Amorous, and made him the hero of his piece.

Sir Bash. What, put him into a comedy!

Sir Bril. Ha! ha! yes, he has; it is called the
Amorous Huſband, or the Man in Love with his own
wife—I muſt be there the firſt night. Sir Baſhful,
you ſhall be of our party.

Sir Bash. It will be a very agreeable party.—I
ſhall enjoy the joke prodigiouſly—ha! ha!
(*Forcing a laugh.*)

Sir Bril. It will be the higheſt ſcene in nature—
well!—a good day, Sir Baſhful—I muſt drive to a
thouſand places, and put it about—farewel! let my
lady know this affair—it will appear ſo ridiculous to
her.———

Sir Bash. Do you think it will?———

Sir Bril. O! without doubt—adieu!—Poor Sir
Amorous! He will have his horns added to his coat
of arms in a little time—ha! ha!   (*Exit.*)

Sir BASHFUL alone.

I ſee how it is—I ſhall get lampooned, be-rhymed,
and niched into a comedy—Heaven be praiſed! no
body knows of my affection but Mr. Lovemore,
and he can't diſcover againſt me for his own ſake—
Well!—well Mr. Lovemore!

Enter LOVEMORE.

Sir Bash. Well!—how!—how!—how have you
managed it?

Love. Juſt as I could wiſh; ſhe is infinitely
obliged to me, and will never forget this civility.

Sir Bash. A thouſand thanks to you—She ſuſ-
pects nothing of my being privy to it———

Love. Not the leaſt inkling of it—She talked at
firſt

firft fomething about delicacy, and thought it rather
an indecorum, to accept of money even from me,
who am fo intimate in the family—But that argument was foon filenced—I told her I could not but
fee what a bad hufband you are———

Sir BASH. That was well faid—it had its effect I
hope———

LOVE. Why, I hope it had, and then I talked a
few fentences to her, as that a perfon receiving a civility confers the obligation; that I was fure of
wheedling you in fome unguarded moment to repay
me, and therefore that it was but making you my
banker for a fhort time, with more jargon to that
purpofe; and fo with fome reluctance fhe complied,
and things are now fettled upon as good a footing
as I could wifh.—Death and rage! there's my wife—

Sir BASH. Ay! and there is my wife too.———

LOVE. What the devil brings her hither? (*Afide.*)

Sir BASH. Now let me fee how he will carry it
before Mrs. Lovemore. (*Afide.*) Walk in, walk in,
Mrs. Lovemore.

Enter Mrs. LOVEMORE *and Lady* CONSTANT
at oppofite doors.

Lady CON. Mrs. Lovemore!—I am glad to fee
you abroad, Ma'am.

Mrs. LOVE. I am highly fortunate in meeting
your ladyfhip at home—Mr. Lovemore, I am glad
to fee you, Sir.

LOVE. Mrs. Lovemore, I thank you.

Sir BASH. Ay! ay! mind him now.—(*Afide.*)

Mrs. LOVE. I thought you was gone into the
city, Mr. Lovemore.

LOVE. Why will you mind me, Mrs. Lovemore?
—I deferred going till evening.———

Mrs. LOVE. Then I may hope you will dine at
home, Sir.

LOVE. Oh! Lord! how can you teaze a man fo?

Sir

Sir Bash. Yes, yes; I fee how it is; he won't let her have the leaft fufpicion of his regard—

(Afide.)

Lady Con. No doubt Mr. Lovemore will dine at home, if it will give you any fatisfaction, Ma'am; and Sir Bafhful will dine at home, I reckon, for the contrary reafon.

Sir Bash. Madam, I will dine at home, or I will dine abroad, for what reafon I pleafe—I am my own mafter, Madam,—Lovemore, fhe little fufpects me. (*Afide and laughing.*)

Love. Not the leaft—What a filly blockhead it is—ha! ha! (*Afide.*)

Mrs. Love. I fee your chariot is at the door, Mr. Lovemore; I'll fend away my chair, and you may fet me down———

Love. Ma'am, I have feveral places to call at.

Sir Bash. Cunning! cunning!—He would not be feen in a chariot with her for the world. (*Afide.*)

Lady Con. I am to have a rout to-morrow evening, Mrs. Lovemore—I wifh you would favour us with your company.

Sir Bash. A rout to morrow evening!—you have a rout every evening, I think———I wifh, Madam, you would learn of Mrs. Lovemore, and not make a fool of me as you do—hip! Lovemore. (*Afide ; they both laugh.*)

Love. Well! I muft be gone—My lady Conftant, I have the honour to wifh your ladyfhip a good morning—I beg you will take no notice to Sir Bafhful—Ma'am your moft obedient———(*bows obfequioufly to her.*) Sir Bafhful yours—Madam———

(Bows gravely to Mrs. Lovemore, and exit.)

Sir Bash. He carries it off finely———I have kept my own fecret too, and fhe fhall never know it.——— Mrs. Lovemore, your moft obedient fervant, Madam—(*bows complaifantly*) Madam———(*to Lady Conftant*) (*bows gravely, and exit.*)

Mrs.

Mrs. LOVEMORE *and Lady* CONSTANT.

Mrs. Love. Two such husbands!

Lady Con. As to my swain, Mrs. Lovemore, I grant you—but you may set your mind at rest ; Mr. Lovemore is at least well-bred, whereas Sir Bashful never qualifies his disrespect with the least tincture of civility.

Mrs. Love. If there is any pleasure in being made miserable with civility, I must allow Mr. Lovemore a most skilful hand. I have found out another of his intrigues, and I came on purpose to consult with your ladyship about it.—There is a widow Bellmour to whom he now pays his addresses.

Lady Con. The widow Bellmour!

Mrs. Love. Yes; and Sir Brilliant Fashion, to cover the affair, has been giving her a most perfect character.

Lady Con. Why, Sir Brilliant's authority is in general not the best—But in this point he is right, I assure you————

Mrs. Love. Give me leave however to explain to you the whole circumstances of the affair.————

Lady Con. But, my dear Ma'am, I know her so well————

Mrs. Love. Nay, give me the hearing; I am afraid there is too much in it, and I am determined to search it to the bottom.

Lady Con. All scandal, take my word for it— But if I must hear your story, let us adjourn the debate to my dressing-room, and I will promise to confute your whole accusation—My dear Mrs. Lovemore, are you not tending a little towards jealousy ? —beware of that, Ma'am; you must not look thro' that medium ;

That jaundice of the mind, whose colours strike
On friend and foe, and paint them all alike.

End of the Second Act.

❀❀❀❀❀❀❀❀❀❀ ❀❀❀❀❀❀❀❀❀❀

A C T   III.

SCENE, *a Room at Mr.* LOVEMORE's.

Mr. and Mrs. LOVEMORE *discovered at Table;
servants attending.*

LOVEMORE.

I Wonder you are not tired, Mrs. Lovemore, of this eternal topic.—William, reach me a tooth-pick——

WIL. Yes, Sir.

Mrs. LOVE. If I make it an eternal topic, as you call it, Sir, I am sure it is for your good, Mr. Lovemore.

LOVE. I thank you, Ma'am——I know I always have your good wishes, and *(picking his teeth)* you have my good wishes, Mrs. Lovemore.

Mrs. LOVE. If you would but wish well to yourself, Sir, I should be happy—But your health must be ruined, Mr. Lovemore, in the way you go on ;—I wonder how you hold it out at all, Sir—your appetite is quite gone ; you have not eat a morsel of dinner.

LOVE. Don't say so, my dear, *(picking his teeth)* don't say so ; I have done very well.

Mrs. LOVE. Pardon me, Sir ; I took notice ; and how should it be otherwise ?—In your course of life the whole order of things is inverted ; night is day, and day is night ; your substance squandered, your constitution destroyed, your spirits exhausted, and your family-concerns quite neglected.

LOVE. Here's all our absent friends, Mrs. Lovemore, *(drinks.)*

Mrs. LOVE. And, at the rate you go on, every thing must go to ruin ;—a tavern-life !—I wonder what

what pleasure you can find in a tavern-life !——The
gaming table, riot, and dissipation—Company about
you, that I know your good sense must despise, not
to mention that coldness and neglect, which I meet
with in consequence of all this—(*During this speech,*
Lovemore *wets the corner of a napkin, rubs his teeth,
and looks with a gay indifference at her*)—I am not
conscious how I have merited this treatment, Mr.
Lovemore.—will you answer me one question ?——

Love. With pleasure, Ma'am.

Mrs. Love. Lay your hand on your heart, and
tell me then,—have I deserved this usage ?

Love. My dear life (*takes some water in his mouth,
and stares at her.*)

Mrs. Love. Answer me that, Sir, and answer me
sincerely.

Love. William, take all these things away—

Wil. Yes, Sir !——

Love. And reach that arm-chair, I don't sit easy
here ; ay ! this will do—(*composes himself, with his
back turned to her*) (*Exeunt servants.*)

Mrs. Love. I say, Mr. Lovemore, I think I have
been no way deficient in setting a proper value upon
you. You won my heart, and I freely gave it to
you ;—from that moment, Sir, I have never abated
from the love I bore you, whatever you may have
done on your part——

Love. (*going to sleep.*) It is very true, my dear.

Mrs. Love. Your interest has been mine ; your
houshold affairs have been the object of my attention ;
diversions, high living, shew, and idle pomp, have
never had allurements for me—

Love. (*endeavouring to keep his eyes open.*) I can't
contradict you, my dear.

Mrs. Love. Had I been inclined to imitate the example of many other women, you might have been
thousands out of pocket by this time ; and tho' the
fortune I brought you might entitle me to pleasur-

able

able expences, yet œconomy and the domeſtic duties
of a wife (Lovemore *drops aſleep*) were more power-
ful motives with me—Some women conſider marriage as an introduction to the great ſcene of the world;
I rather thought it a ſober and chearful retreat to leſs
noiſy and ſerener pleaſures.   What is called polite
company I never delighted in, ſince marriage made
me yours; the pleaſure ariſing from your company,
Mr. Lovemore—Upon my word, I have great reaſon to be charmed with his company—Faſt aſleep!—
This is ever his way—inſenſible man!—It is too plain
that I am grown loathſome to him, and miſery muſt
be my portion.—Mr. Lovemore!—Mr. Lovemore!
——If you knew what affliction you occaſion in this
heart, you would hardly find it in your nature to
treat me thus—I will not diſturb him, and yet I
cannot tamely ſubmit to be unhappy.   This affair
of the widow Bellmour, I will trace to the bottom
—Lady Conſtant is laviſh in her praiſe; then I may
ſafely adventure upon this viſit;—I'll ſtep to my
chair this inſtant, and at all events, I will undertake
it—Oh! Mr. Lovemore!—my heart will break at
laſt—— (*Exit.*)

Lovemore *talks in his ſleep; his head nodding about.*

No, my dear, no;—I an't aſleep;—it was not ſo
late—at home by two o'clock—(*ſleeps and nods.*) I do
liſten—you are very right in all you ſay—I am only
a little thoughtful——(*ſleeps and mutters indiſtinct
words*) no—no—no—no ſuch thing — Sir Baſhful
Conſtant is a fooliſh fellow—no, my dear, no no—
(*ſleeps and his head rolls about violently*) zoons! I am
ready to drop aſleep — I beg your pardon, Mrs.
Lovemore; what did you ſay, my dear? (*leans on
the table without looking about*) To be ſure what you
ſay is very true; but one cannot always, you know,
my dear (*turning about.*) 'Sdeath! She is gone—oh!
Lord! I fell faſt aſleep—let me ſhake off this drowſy
(*riſes*)

(rises)—I dined at home for want of knowing how to diſpoſe of myſelf abroad, and thus I am over-taken—What's o'clock ? — Six—William, get rea-dy; I am going out directly.——Now to buſineſs; are my people ready there?————

WIL. *(within.)* Yes, Sir; all ready————

LOVE. Very well; I am coming; and now, my dear Madam Venus, with more rapture than any of your votaries felt, I now invoke you—I make but a ſlight requeſt; quit your Cyprian iſle, and attend me this afternoon;

————Your beſt arms employ,
All wing'd with pleaſure, and all tipt with joy.
(Exit.)

SCENE, *a Room at the Widow* Bellmour's, *in which are diſpoſed up and down, ſeveral Chairs, a Toilette, a Book-caſe, and a Harpſicord;* Mignionet *her maid, is ſettling the Toilette.*

Enter Mrs. Bellmour, *reading a Volume of* Pope.

Oh ! bleſt with temper, whoſe unclouded ray,
Can make to-morrow, chearful as to-day;
She who can own a ſiſter's charms, and hear
Sighs for a daughter, with unwounded ear;
That never anſwers till a huſband cools,
And if ſhe rules him, never ſhews ſhe rules;

Senſible, elegant Pope !

Charms by accepting, by ſubmitting ſways,
Yet has her humour moſt when ſhe obeys;
(ſeems to read on.

MIG. Lord love my miſtreſs !—She's always ſo happy, and ſo gay.————

Mrs. BELL. Theſe charming characters of women ! —'Tis like a painter's gallery, where one ſees the
por-

portraits of all one's acquaintance !——Here, Mignionet, put this book in its place.

Mig. Yes, Ma'am.——There, Ma'am, you fee
your toilette looks moſt charmingly.

Mrs. Bell. Does it ?—I think it does.—A propos,
where's my new fong ?—Here it lies,—I muſt make
myſelf miſtreſs of it.—(Plays and ſings a little.)—I
believe I ſhall conquer it preſently, (riſes and goes towards her toilette)—This hair of mine is always tor-
menting me ;—always in diſorder, and ſtraggling
out of its place :—I muſt abſolutely ſubdue this
lock.—Mignionet, do you know that this is a very
pretty fong ?——'tis written by my lord Etheridge ;
——I poſitively muſt learn it before he comes.——
(Sings a line)—Do you know, Mignionet, that I
think my lord not wholly intolerable?

Mig. Yes, Ma'am, I know that.

Mrs. Bell. Do you ?

Mig. And if I have any ſkill, Ma'am, I fancy
you think him more than tolerable.

Mrs. Bell. Really ! then you think I like him,
I ſuppoſe.—Do ye think I like him ?—I don't well
know how that is,—and yet I don't know but I do
like him ;—no,—no,—I don't like him neither,—
not abſolutely like ;—but I could like, if I had a
mind to humour myſelf.—The man has a ſoftneſs of
manner, an elegant turn of thinking, and has a
heart—has he a heart?—yes, I think he has ;——
and then he is ſuch an obſerver of the manners,—
and ſhews the ridiculous of them with ſo much humour—

Mig. I'll be whipt, if you don't get into the
nooſe before the long nights are over. — Without
doubt, Ma'am, my lord is a pretty man enough ;
but lack a day what o'that ?—You know but very
little of him.—your acquaintance is but very ſhort ;
—(Mrs. Bellmour hums a tune) do, pray my dear
Madam, mind what I ſay,—for I am at times I aſ-

ſure

affure you, very fpeculative,—very fpeculative indeed;—and I fee very plainly. — Lord, Ma'am,
what am I doing!—I am talking to you for your
own good, and you're all in the air, and no more
mind me, no, no more, than if I was nothing at
all.

Mrs. Bell. *(Hums a tune ftill.)* Why indeed you
talk wonderfully well upon the fubject; but as I
know how the cards lie, and can play the game myfelf, and as I don't know my fong,—why a-body is
inclined to give that the preference. *(Sings.)*

Mig. Ma'am, I affure you, I am none of thofe
fervants that bargain for their miftrefs's inclinations;
—but I fee you are going to take a leap in the dark.
—I don't know what to make of his manner of coming here, with his chair always brought into the hall,
and the curtains drawn clofe about his ears, as if —
May I never be married, if I don't believe there is
fomething amifs in the affair.—Dear heart, Ma'am,
if you won't liften to me, what fignifies my living
with you?—I am of no fervice to you.———

Mrs. Bell. I believe I have conquered the fong;
—*(Runs to her glafs,)* how do I look to-day?—Well
enough, I think. — Do you think I fhall play the
fool, Mignionet, and marry my Lord?

Mig. You have it, Ma'am, thro' the very heart
of you—I fee that.

Mrs. Bell. Do you think fo?—May be I may
marry, and may be not.—Poor Sir Brilliant Fafhion,
—what will become of him? But I won't think
about it.

Enter POMPEY.

Mrs. Bell. What's the matter, Pompey?

Pom. There's a lady below in a chair, that defires to know if you are at home, Madam.

Mrs. Bell. Has the lady no name?

Pom. She did not tell her name.

H

Mrs.

Mrs. Bell. How aukward you are !—Well shew her up. (*Exit* Pompey.

Mig. Had not you better receive the lady in the dining-room, Ma'am ? — Things here are in such confusion.———

Mrs. Bell. No, it will do very well here.. I dare say it is some body I am intimate with, tho' the boy does not recollect her name.—Here she comes.

Enter Mrs. LOVEMORE.

(They both look with a grave surprize at each other, then curtsey with an air of distant civility.)

Mrs. Bell. Ma'am, your most obedient,—*(with a kind of reserve.)*

Mrs. Love. Ma'am, I beg your pardon for this intrusion.—*(disconcerted)*

Mrs. Bell. Pray Ma'am walk in,———won't you please to be seated?—Mignionet reach a chair. (*Mrs. Lovemore crosses the stage, and they salute each other.*

Mrs. Love. I'm afraid this visit from one unknown to you, will be inconvenient and troublesome.

Mrs. Bell. Not at all, I dare say ;—you need not be at the trouble of an apology :—would you chuse a dish of chocolate ?

Mrs. Love. I am much oblig'd to you, Ma'am ; not any.

Mrs. Bell. Mignionet, you may withdraw.

(*Exit* Mignionet.)

Mrs. Love. Tho' I have not the pleasure of your acquaintance, Ma'am, there is a particular circumstance which has determin'd me to take this liberty with you ; for which I intreat your pardon beforehand.

Mrs. Bell. The request is wholly unnecessary ;—but a particular circumstance, you say———Pray Ma'am to what circumstance am I indebted for this honour ?

Mrs.

Mrs. Love. I fhall appear perhaps very ridiculous, and indeed I am afraid I have done the moft abfurd thing.—But Ma'am, a lady of your acquaintaince, My lady Conftant———

Mrs. Bell. My lady Conftant!—I know her very well———.

Mrs. Love. She, Ma'am, has given you fuch an amiable character, that I eafily incline to flatter myfelf, you will not take offence at any thing; and that if it is in your power, you will afford me your affiftance.

Mrs. Bell. You may depend upon me.

Mrs. Love. I will be very ingenuous; — Pray Ma'am, an't you acquainted with a gentleman whofe name is Lovemore?

Mrs. Bell. Lovemore!—No,—no fuch perfon in my lift.—Lovemore!—I don't know him, Ma'am.

Mrs. Love. Ma'am, I beg your pardon—I am but where I was.—I won't trouble you any farther, *(going.)*

Mrs. Bell. 'Tis mighty odd, this *(afide.)* Madam I muft own my curiofity is a good deal excited; —*(Takes her by the hand.)*—Pray Ma'am, give me leave—I beg you will fit down,—pray don't think me impertinent—may I beg to know who the gentleman is?

Mrs. Love. The fubject will be uninterefting to you, and to me it is too painful—My tears will force their way———*(cries.)*

Mrs. Bell. Tears! her grief foftens me ftrangely —I beg you will explain, Ma'am.

Mrs. Love. You are very obliging, Ma'am, and I will endeavour—I have been married thefe two years; I admired my hufband for his underftanding, his fentiment, and fpirit; I thought myfelf as fincerely loved by him, as my fond heart could wifh, but there is of late, fuch a ftrange revolution in his temper, I know not what to make of it :—inftead of

H 2 the

the looks of affection, and expreffions of tendernefs
with which he ufed to meet me, 'tis nothing now but
cold, averted, fuperficial civility.——While abroad he
runs on in a wild career of pleafure; and to my deep
affliction, has fix'd his affections upon another object.

Mrs. BELL. If you mean to confult with me in regard to this cafe, I am afraid you have made a wrong
choice; there is fomething in her appearance that af-
fects me, (afide.)——Pray excufe me, Ma'am, you
confider this matter too deeply.——Men will prove
falfe, and if there is nothing in your complaint but
mere gallantry on his fide,——upon my word, I can't
think your cafe the worfe for that.

Mrs. LOVE. Not the worfe!

Mrs. BELL. On the contrary, much better. If
his affections, inftead of being alienated, had been
extinguifh'd, he would have funk into a downright
ftupid, habitual infenfibility; from which it might
prove impoffible to recal him.——In all love's bill of
mortality there is not a more fatal diforder,——but
your hufband is not fallen into that way.——By your
account, he ftill has fentiment, and where there is fentiment, there is ftill room to hope for an alteration.——
But in the other cafe, you have the pain of feeing
yourfelf neglected, and for what?——for nothing at
all;——the man has loft all fenfe of feeling, and is become to the warm beams of wit and beauty, as im-
penetrable as an ice-houfe.

Mrs. LOVE. I am afraid, Ma'am, he is too much
the reverfe of this, too fufceptible of impreffions from
every beautiful object.

Mrs. BELL. Why, fo much the better, as I told
you already;——fome new idea has ftruck his fancy,
and he will be for a while, under the influence of
that.

Mrs. LOVE. How light fhe makes of it! (afide.)

Mrs. BELL. But it is the wife's bufinefs to bait the
hook for her hufband with variety; and to draw him
daily

daily to herself:— that is the whole affair, I would not make myself uneasy, Ma'am.

Mrs. Love. Not uneasy! when his indifference does not diminish my regard for him! Not uneasy, when the man I doat on, no longer fixes his happiness at home!

Mrs. Bell. Ma'am, you'll give me leave to speak my mind freely.—I have often observ'd, when the fiend jealousy is rous'd, that women lay out a wonderful deal of anxiety and vexation to no account, when perhaps, if the truth were known, they shou'd be angry with themselves instead of their husbands.

Mrs. Love. Angry with myself, Madam!—— calumny can lay nothing to my charge,—the virtue of my conduct, Madam——

Mrs. Bell. Look ye there now,—I wou'd have laid my life, you wou'd be at that work—that's the folly of us all.—But virtue is out of the question at present.—I mean the want of address, and proper management! It is there that most women fail,— virtue alone cannot please the taste of this age.—It is *La Belle Nature*,—Nature embellished by the advantages of art, that the men expect now-a-days.

Mrs. Love. But after being married so long, and behaving all that time with such an equality——

Mrs. Bell. Ay, that equality is the rock so many split upon.—The men are now so immers'd in luxury, that they must have eternal variety in their happiness.

Mrs. Love. She justifies him.   (*Aside.*)

Mrs. Bell. I'll tell you what; I wou'd venture to lay a pot of coffee, that the person who now rivals you in your husband's affection, does it without your good qualities, and even without your beauty, by the mere force of agreeable talents, and affiduity to please.

Mrs. Love. I am afraid that compliment——

Mrs.

Mrs. Bell. Let me afk you, Ma'am, have you ever feen this formidable perfon?

Mrs. Love. There I own I am puzzled.

Mrs. Bell. What fort of a woman, pray?

Mrs. Love. Formidable indeed!—She was defcrib'd to me as one of charming, and rare accomplifhments.

Mrs. Bell. Never throw up the cards for all that.—Really, Ma'am, without compliment, you feem to have all the qualities that can difpute your hufband's heart with any body; but the exertion of thofe qualities, I am afraid, is fuppref'd.—You'll excufe my freedom.—You fhou'd counterwork your rival, by the very fame art fhe employs.—I know a lady now in your very fituation,—and what does fhe do? She confumes herfelf with eternal jealoufy; whereas, if fhe wou'd but employ half the pains fhe ufes in teazing herfelf, to vie with the creature that has won her hufband from her,—to vie with her, I fay, in the arts of pleafing,—for it is there a woman's pride fhou'd be piqued,—wou'd fhe do that, take my word for it, victory wou'd declare in her favour.

Mrs. Love. Do you think fo, Ma'am?

Mrs. Bell. Think fo!—I am fure of it.—Virtue alone, by her own native charms wou'd do, if men were perfect; but that is not the cafe, and fince vice can affume allurements, why fhould not truth and innocence have additional ornaments alfo?

Mrs. Love. I find Sir Brilliant told me truth.

(*Afide.*)

Mrs. Bell. I have been married, Ma'am, and am a little in the fecret.—It is much more difficult to keep a heart than win one—After the fatal words " for better for worfe," the general way with wives is to relax into indolence, and while they are guilty of no infidelity, they think that is enough:—but they are miftaken, there is a great deal wanting—an addrefs, a manner, a defire of pleafing—an agreeable

2   able

able contraſt in their conduct, of grave, and gay;
—a favourite poet of mine—Prior, has expreſſed
this very delicately.

Above the fix'd and ſettled rules
Of vice, and virtue, in the ſchools,
The better part ſhould ſet before 'em
A grace, a manner, a decorum.

Mrs. Love. But when the natural temper—

Mrs. Bell. The natural temper muſt be forc'd,
home muſt be made a place of pleaſure to the huſband, and the wife muſt throw infinite variety into
her manner;—in ſhort, ſhe muſt, as it were, mul-
tiply herſelf, and appear to him ſundry different women on different occaſions.—And this, I take to be
the whole myſtery; the way to keep a man.—But I
run on at a ſtrange rate.—Well, to be ſure, I'm the
giddieſt creature.—Ma'am, will you now give me
leave to enquire, how I came to have this favour?
Who recommended me to your notice?—And pray
who was ſo kind as to intimate that I was acquainted
with Mr. Lovemore?

Mrs. Love. I beg your pardon for all the
trouble I have given you, and I aſſure you, 'tis entirely owing to my being told that his viſits were frequent here.

Mrs. Bell. His viſits frequent here! My lady
Conſtant could not ſay that—

Mrs. Love. No, Ma'am; quite the reverſe; ſhe
aſſured me you would make me eaſy on that head—

Mrs. Bell. Then I find ſcandal has been buz-
zing about; but, I aſſure you, I do not know the
gentleman.——Oh! lud, I hear a rap at the door,
I poſitively won't be at home. *(Rings a bell.)*

Enter MIGNIONET,

Mign. Did you call, Madam?
Mrs. Bell. I am not at home.

MIGN.

MIGN. 'Tis lord Etheridge, Ma'am,—he's coming up ſtairs, the ſervants told him you were within.

Mrs. BELL. Was ever any thing ſo croſs? Tell him there is company with me, and he won't come in. Mignionet, run to him.

Mrs. LOVE. Ma'am, I beg I mayn't hinder you.

Mrs. BELL. Our converſation begins to grow intereſting, and I wou'd not have you go for the world. I won't ſee my lord.

Mrs. LOVE. I beg you will, don't let me prevent, I'll ſtep into another room.

Mrs. BELL. Will you be ſo kind?—There is a ſtudy of books in that room, if you will be ſo obliging as to amuſe yourſelf there, I ſhall be glad to reſume this converſation again.—He ſhan't ſtay long.

Mrs. LOVE. I beg you will be in no hurry, I can wait with pleaſure.

Mrs. BELL. This is a lover of mine; and a huſband and a lover ſhou'd be treated in the ſame manner; perhaps it will divert you to hear how I manage him. I hear him on the ſtairs, for heaven's ſake, make haſte. Mignionet, ſhew the way.

MIGN. This way, Madam, this way.

(*Exeunt Mrs.* Love, *and* Mignionet.)

Mrs. BELL. Let me ſee how I look to receive him. (*Runs to her glaſs.*)

Enter LOVEMORE, *with a Star and Ribband as Lord* ETHERIDGE.

Mrs. BELL. (*Looking in her glaſs.*) Lord Etheridge! Walk in, my Lord.

LOVE. (*Repeats.*)

A heav'nly image in the glaſs appears,
To that ſhe bends, to that her eyes ſhe rears,
Repairs her ſmiles——

Mrs.

Mrs. Bell. Repairs her smiles, my Lord! I don't like your application of that phrase—Pray, my Lord, are my smiles out of repair, like an old house in the country, that wants a tenant?

Love. Nay now, that's wresting the words from their visible intention.—You can't suppose I thought you want repair, whatever may be the case, Ma'am, with regard to the want of a tenant.

Mrs. Bell. And so you think I really want a tenant! And perhaps you imagine too, that I am going to put up a bill, *(Looking in her glass)* to signify to all passers-by, that here is a mansion to be let.—Well, I swear, I don't think it wou'd be a bad scheme.—I have a great mind to do so.

Love. And he who has the preference—

Mrs. Bell. Will be very happy, I know you mean so. But I'll let it to none but a single gentleman, that you may depend upon.

Love. What the devil does she mean by that? She has not got an inkling of the affair, I hope. *(Aside.)* None else could presume, Madam, to—

Mrs. Bell. And then it must be a lease for life, —But nobody will be troubled with it—I shall never get it off my hands.—Do you think I shall, my Lord?

Love. Why that question, Madam? You know I am devoted to you, even if it were to be bought with life.

Mrs. Bell. Heav'ns! what a dying swain you are! And does your lordship really intend to be guilty of matrimony?—Lord, what a question have I asked?—Well, to be sure, I am a very mad-cap! —My Lord, don't you think me a strange mad-cap?

Love. A wildness like yours, that arises from vivacity and sentiment together, serves only to exalt your beauty, and give new poignancy to every charm.

Mrs. Bell. Well, upon my word you have said it finely!—But you are in the right, my Lord.—I

I   hate

hate your penfive, melancholy beauty, that fits like a well-grown vegetable in a room for an hour to-gether, 'till at laft fhe is animated to the violent ex-ertion of faying yes or no, and then enters into a matter-of-fact converfation, "Have you heard the the news? Mifs Beverly is going to be married to captain Shoulderknot. My lord Mortgage has had another tumble at Arthur's. Sir William Squander-ftock has loft his election. They fay, fhort aprons are coming into fashion again."

Love. Oh, lord! a matter-of-fact converfation is infupportable.

Mrs. Bell. Pray, my lord, have you ever ob-ferved the manner of one lady's accofting another at Ranelagh?—She comes up to you with a demure look of infipid ferenity,—makes you a folemn falute —" Ma'am, I am overjoyed to meet you,—you look charmingly.—But, dear Madam, did you hear what happened to us all the other night?—— We were going home from the Opera, Ma'am; —you know my aunt Roly-Poly,—it was her coach, —there was fhe,—and lady Betty Fidget,—Your moft obedient fervant, Ma'am, (*Curtfeying to another, as it were going by*) lady Betty, you know, is recovered—every body thought it over with her, —but doctor Snakeroot was called in, no not doctor Snakeroot, Doctor Bolus it was, and fo he altered the courfe of the medicines,—and fo my lady Betty recovered;—well, there was fhe and Sir George Bragwell,—a pretty man Sir George,—fineft teeth in the world.—Your Ladyfhip's moft obedient.— We expected you laft night,—but you did not come, he! he!—And fo there was he and the reft of us,— and fo turning the corner of Bond-ftreet, the vil-lain of a coachman—How do you do, Madam?— The villain of a coachman overturned us all;— my aunt Roly-Poly, was frightened out of her wits,

wits, and lady Betty has been nervish ever since :—
Only think of that,—such accidents in life.—Ma'am
your moſt obedient,—I am proud to ſee you look
ſo well."

Love. An exact deſcription,—the very thing—
ha! ha!

Mrs. Bell. And then from this converſation they
all run to cards,—" Quadrille has murdered wit."

Love. Ay, and beauty too; for upon theſe occaſions, " the paſſions in the features are—" I
have ſeen many a beautiful countenance change in a
moment, into abſolute deformity; the little loves
and graces that before ſparkled in the eye, bloom'd
in the cheek, and ſmil'd about the mouth, all fly
off in an inſtant, and reſign the features which they
before adorn'd, to fear, to anger, to grief, and the
whole train of fretful paſſions.

Mrs. Bell. Ay, and the rage we poor women
are often betrayed into on theſe occaſions—

Love. Very true, Ma'am; and if by chance,
they do bridle and hold in a little, the ſtruggle they
undergo is the moſt ridiculous ſight imaginable.—
I have ſeen an oath quivering upon the pale lip of a
reigning toaſt, for half an hour together; yes, and
I have ſeen an uplifted eye blaſpheming providence
for the loſs of an odd trick ;—and then at laſt, when
the whole room burſt out into one loud univerſal
uproar, " My Lord, you flung away the game.—
No, Ma'am, it was you.—Sir George, why did
not you rough the diamond ? Capt. Hazard, why
did not you lead through the honour ? Ma'am, it
was not the play.—Pardon me, Sir,—But Ma'am,
—But Sir,—I would not play with you for ſtraws.
Don't you know what Hoyle ſays ? If A and B are
partners againſt C and D, and the game nine-all,
A and B have won three tricks, and C and D four
tricks; C leads his ſuit, D puts up the king then
returns the ſuit, A paſſes, C puts up the queen, B

roughs

ᵗoughs the next :" and ſo A and B, and C and D
are bang'd about ; and all is jargon, confuſion, uproar, and wrangling, and nonſenſe, and noiſe.—
Ha! ha!

Mrs. BELL. Ha! ha! A fine picture of a rout ;
but one muſt play ſometimes—we muſt let our
friends pick our pockets ſometimes, or they'll drop
our acquaintance.—Pray, my Lord, do you never
play ?

LOVE. Play, Ma'am !—I muſt lie to the end of
the chapter, (*Aſide*,) play !—now and then out of
neceſſity ;—otherwiſe,—I never touch a card.

Mrs. BELL. Oh! very true, you dedicate your
time to the muſes ; a downright rhyming Peer.—
Do you know, my Lord, that I am charm'd with
your ſong ?

LOVE. Are you ?

Mrs. BELL. I am indeed ;—I think you'd make
a very tolerable Vauxhall poet.

LOVE. you flatter me, Ma'am.

Mrs. BELL. No, as I live and breathe, I don't ;
—and do you know that I can ſing it already ?—
Come, you ſhall hear me,—you ſhall hear it. (*Sings.*)

I.

Attend all ye fair, and I'll tell ye the art
  To bind every fancy with eaſe in your chains,
To hold in ſoft fetters the conjugal heart,
  And baniſh from Hymen his doubts and his pains.

II.

When Juno accepted the ceſtus of love,
  At firſt ſhe was handſome ; ſhe charming became ;
With skill the ſoft paſſions it taught her to move,
  To kindle at once, and to keep up the flame.

III.

'Tis this gives the eyes all their magic and fire ;
  The voice melting accents ; impaſſions the kiſs ;
Confers the ſweet ſmiles that awaken deſire,
  And plants round the fair each incentive to bliſs.

IV.

IV.

Thence flows the gay chat, more than reason that
    charms;
  The eloquent blush, that can beauty improve;
The fond sigh, the fond vow, the soft touch that alarms,
  The tender disdain, the renewal of love.

V.

Ye fair take the cestus, and practise its art;
  The mind unaccomplish'd, mere features are vain,
Exert your sweet pow'r, you will conquer each heart,
  And the loves, joys and graces, shall walk in your
    train.

Love. My poetry is infinitely oblig'd to you, for the embellishments your voice and manner confer upon it.

Mrs. Bell. O fulsome!—I sing horridly, and I look horridly; *(goes to the glass)*—How do I look, my Lord?—but don't tell me,—I won't be told.—I see you are studying a compliment, and I hate compliments;—well, what is it? let's hear your compliment—why don't you compliment me?—I won't hear it now.—But pray now how came you to choose so grave a subject as connubial happiness?——

Love. Close and particular that question; *(Aside.)*

Mrs. Bell. Well upon my word you have drawn your picture so well in this little song, that one would imagine you had a wife at home to sit for it.

Love. Ma'am, *(embarrass'd)* the compliment,—a—you are but laughing at me;—I—I,—I—Zounds, I am afraid she begins to smoke me, *(Aside.)*—A very scanty knowledge of the world will serve: and —and there is no need of one's own experience in these cases:—and when you, Madam, are the original, it is no wonder that this copy——

Mrs. Bell. O lard, you are going to plague me again with your odious solicitations, but I won't hear 'em;—you must be gone.—If I should be

weak

weak enough to listen to you, what would become
of Sir Brilliant Fashion?

Love. Sir Brilliant Fashion!

Mrs. Bell. Yes, don't you know Sir Brilliant
Fashion?

Love. No, Ma'am, I don't know the gentleman:—I beg pardon if he is your acquaintance, but
from what I have heard of him, I should not chuse
him to be among my intimates.

Enter MIGNIONET *in a violent hurry.*

Mign. O lud! I am frighted out of my senses,
—The poor lady.—Where's the hartshorn-drops?—

Love. The lady! What lady?

Mign. Never stand asking what lady,—she has
fainted away, Ma'am, all of a sudden. Give me the
drops.—

Mrs. Bell. Let me run to her assistance.—Adieu,
my Lord,—I shall be at home in the evening ;——
Mignionet, step this way.—My Lord, you'll excuse
me ; I expect you in the evening.   (*Exit.*)

Love. I shall wait on you, Ma'am.   What a villain am I to carry on this scheme, against so much
beauty, innocence, and merit?—Ay, and to have
the impudence to assume this badge of honour, to
cover the most unwarrantable purposes !—But no reflection, have her I must ; and that quickly too.—
If I don't prevail soon, I am undone—she'll find me
out :—egad, I'll be with her betimes this evening,
and press her with all the vehemence of love.—Women have their soft, unguarded moments, and who
knows ?—But to take the advantage of the openness
and gaity of her heart !—And then my friend Sir Brilliant, will it be fair to supplant him?—Prithee be
quiet, my dear conscience; don't you be meddling ;
don't you interrupt a gentleman in his amusements.
Don't you know, my good friend, that love has no
respect of persons, knows no laws of friendship ;—
be-

befides, 'tis all my wife's fault—why don't fhe ftrive
to make home agreeable ?

> *For foreign pleafures, foreign joy, I roam,*
> *No thought of peace or happinefs at home.—*

(going.)

(Sir Brilliant *is heard finging within)*

What the devil is Madam Fortune at now ?—Sir
Brilliant, by all that's odious !—No place to conceal
in !—No efcape !—the door is lock'd !—Mignionet,
Mignionet, open the door.

Mign. *(within)* You can't come in here, Sir.

Love. This curfed ftar, and this ribband, will
ruin me.—Let me get off this confounded tell-tale
evidence.—*(takes off the ribband in a hurry.)*

Enter Sir BRILLIANT.

Sir Bril. My dear Madam, I moft heartily rejoice—Ha!—Lovemore!

Love. Your flave, Sir Brilliant, your flave, *(Hi-
ding the ftar with his hat.)*

Sir Bril. How is this ? I did not think you had
been acquainted here !

Love. I came to look for you,—I thought to
have found you here ;—and fo I have fcrap'd an acquaintance with the lady, and made it fubfervient
to your purpofes.—I have been giving a great character of you.

Sir Bril. Well, but what's the matter ?—What
are you fumbling about? *(pulls the hat.)*

Love. 'Sdeath have a care !—for heaven's fake—
(crams his handkerchief there.)

Sir Bril. What the devil ails you ?

Love. Taken fo unaccountably,—my old complaint—Sir Brilliant, yours,

Sir Bril. Zouns, Man, you had beft fit down.

Love. Here's a bufinefs,—*(afide,)*—pray let me
pafs ;—my old complaint.—

Sir Bril. what complaint ?

Love.

- Love. I muſt have a ſurgeon,—occaſioned by the ſtroke of a tennis-ball ;—my Lord Rackett's unlucky left hand :—Let me paſs, there is certainly ſomething forming there,—let me paſs.—To be caught is the devil, *(aſide,)* don't name my name, you'll ruin all that I ſaid for you, if you do.—Sir Brilliant, your ſervant.—There is certainly ſomething forming. *(Exit.)*

'. Sir Bril. What can this mean ? I muſt have this explain'd.—Then Mrs. Lovemore's ſuſpicions are right ; I muſt come at the bottom of it,—Ay, ay ; —there is ſomething forming here !—

Enter Mrs. BELLMOUR.

Sir Bril. My dear Mrs. Bellmour.

Mrs. Bell. Heaven's ! What brings you here ?

. Sir Bril. I congratulate with myſelf upon the felicity of meeting you thus at home.

· Mrs. Bell. Your viſit is unſeaſonable, you muſt be gone.

Sir Bril. Madam, I have a thouſand things —

Mrs. Bell. Well, well, another time.

Sir Bril. Of the tendereſt import.

Mrs. Bell. I can't hear you now ;—fly this moment :—I have a lady taken ill in the next room.

Sir Bril. Ay, and you have had a gentleman taken ill here too.

Mrs. Bell. Do you diſpute my will and pleaſure , —fly this inſtant, *(turns him out.)* So I'll make ſure of the door.

Enter Mrs. LOVEMORE, *leaning on* MIGNIONET.

Mign. This way, Madam, here's more air in this room.

Mrs. Bell. How do you find yourſelf, Ma'am ? Pray ſit down.

Mrs.

Mrs. Love. My fpirits were too weak to bear up any longer, againft fuch a fcene of villainy.

Mrs. Bell. Villainy!—What villainy!

Mrs. Love. Of the blackeft dye!—I fee, Madam, you are acquainted with my hufband.

Mrs. Bell. Acquainted with your hufband! *(angrily.)*

Mrs. Love. A moment's patience, That gentleman that was here with you is my hufband.

Mrs. Bell. Lord Etheridge your hufband!

Mrs. Love. Lord Etheridge, as he calls himfelf, and as you have been made to call him alfo, is no other than Mr. Lovemore.

Mrs. Bell. And has he then been bafe enough to affume that title, to enfnare me to my undoing?

Mign. Well, for certain, I believe the devil's in me; I always thought him a fly one.

Mrs. Love. To fee my hufband carrying on this dark bufinefs,—to fee the man I have loved,—the man I have efteem'd,—the man, I am afraid, I muft ftill love, tho' efteem him again I cannot,—to be a witnefs to his complicated wickednefs,—it was too much for fenfibility like mine,—I felt the fhock too feverely,—and funk under it.

Mrs. Bell. I am ready to do the fame myfelf now. I fink into the very ground with amazement. The firft time I ever faw him was at old Mrs. Loveit's,—fhe introduc'd him to me;—the appointment was of her own making.

Mrs. Love. You know her character, I fuppofe, Madam.

Mrs. Bell. She's a woman of fafhion, and fees a great deal of good company.

Mrs. Love. Very capable of fuch an action for all that.

Mrs. Bell. Well, I cou'd never have imagin'd that any woman wou'd be fo bafe as to pafs fuch a

K cheat

cheat upon me. Step this moment, and give orders never to let him within my doors again. (*To her maid, who goes out.*) I am much oblig'd to you, Ma'am, for this vifit. To me it is highly fortunate, but I am forry for your fhare in't, as the difcovery brings you nothing but a conviction of your hufband's bafenefs.

Mrs. Love. I'm determin'd to be no farther uneafy about him, nor will I live a day longer under his roof.

Mrs. Bell. Hold, hold, make no violent refolutions.—You'll excufe me—I can't help feeling for you, and I think this incident may be ftill converted to your advantage.

Mrs. Love. That can never be,—I am loft beyond redemption.

Mrs. Bell. Don't decide that too rafhly.—Come, come, a man is worth thinking a little about, before one throws the hideous thing away for ever. Befides, you have heard his fentiments. Perhaps you are a little to blame yourfelf.—We will talk this matter over coolly. Ma'am, you have fav'd me,—— and I muft now difcharge the obligation.—You fhall ftay and drink tea with me.

Mrs. Love. I can't poffibly do that,—I won't give you fo much trouble.

Mrs. Bell. It will be a pleafure, Ma'am,—you fhall ftay with me, I will not part with you, and I will lay fuch a plan, as may enfure him yours for ever.—Come, come, my dear Madam, don't you ftill think he has fome good qualities to apologize for his vices?

Mrs. Love. I muft own, I ftill hope he has.

Mrs. Bell. Very well then, and he may ftill make atonement for all; and let me tell you, that a man who can make proper atonement for his faults fhould not be entirely defpis'd—Allons! [*Exeunt.*

End of the Third Act.

ACT

A C T IV.

S C E N E, at the Widow BELLMOUR's.

Enter WILLIAM *and* MIGNIONET.

W I L L I A M.

BUT I tell you, Mrs. Mignionet—
MIGN. But I tell you, Mr. Brazen, he is not here—There is no body at home; so rid the house, do; you have no business here.

WIL. Nay, don't be in a passion; did not you hear my Lord give me his orders to come for him?

MIGN. Well, it does not signify; he has been gone this good while; a fine Lord truly!—

WIL. So he is indeed, Mrs. Mignionet;—and very ungrateful you have both been, you and your Lady, to behave in this manner to persons of our dignity.

MIGN. Very well; may be so; but decamp with your dignity, do; follow my Lord, march.—

WIL. Ay! I am going; adieu, Mrs. Mignionet, adieu!—Don't you cry;——don't let me see your tears—I have not so much flint about my heart as I thought—Upon my soul I pity thee; I do indeed, Child—

MIGN. Well! No more of your nonsense, but turn upon your rogue's heel, and rid the house.

WIL. We intended very handsomely by you both; we did, I assure you;—if we had liked ye upon trial; I do in my conscience believe we should have taken ye both into keeping.

MIGN. Don't be vulgar, Mr. Impertinent.—

K 2　　　　　　　　　　　　　　WIL.

Wil. It is my real opinion we fhould have done it—our ufual way indeed is, if we fee a woman we like, " a fine creature that!—fhape, very well !— " air, good !—an eye too !—upon my foul, a deli- " cate, melting, fleepy eye!"——Oh! darts and flames ; we are all on fire ;—" Have fome com- " paffion, thou angel of thy fex, upon a poor dying " fwain that long has—What would the man be at ? " —You don't mean to be rude, Sir ?—no Ma- " dam ; not in the leaft—*tout au contraire*." So up go the heels of her virtue in an inftant ; we revel in delight, furfeit on joys, and then come to our- felves again, make a grave bow, " Ma'am, your " moft obedient," fo cock our hats, hum a tune; walk off with an air, and drop her acquaintance ; that's our ufual way—

Mign. Hold your loofe, profligate, impudent tongue—

Wil. That's our ufual way—but with you,—for really we had fome regard for you,—with you I be- lieve we fhould have proceeded in a different man- ner—it's my opinion, we fhould have let you have a honey-moon out of us at leaft—

Mign. Don't provoke me, you impudent block- head ; don't—

Wil. It begins to work with her—(*afide.*) You would have been both very happy, Mrs. Mignionet, I can tell you that—an agreeable man, my Lord— greatly admired in foreign parts—

Mign. Admired!—I wifh I dare tell him all I know. (*Afide.*)

Wil. And as for me—mind that figure—not well built to be fure ! ha ! ha ! you would have been won- derfully happy—your miftrefs would have been lady Etheridge for the time being ;—and you—

Mign. Hold your tongue, or I'll tear your eyes out, I will—

Wil.

Wil. You fhould have been Madam Ufeful, the
fuppofed wife of William Ufeful, gentleman of the
bed-chamber to the faid lord Etheridge—

Mign. Unmannerly coxcomb!—I could leave the
print of my ten nails upon your rogue's face, I could—
(Runs at him.)

Wil. Moderate your anger, my dear, moderate
your anger—*(holding her.)*

Mign. You impudent blockhead!—

Wil. Softly—

Mign. You unhang'd villain!—

Wil. Don't be furious—all this good we intended
ye both; it would not indeed have lafted for ever;—
the reign of your beauty would in time decline; then
we fhould be for calmly taking our leave, and you, on
your parts, would have tuñed your miferable pipes—
" Will you ferve two poor tender-hearted women in
" this manner? ye crocodiles of the Nile, ye lions
" of the foreft, ye Ruffian bears, ye monfters of the
" defert.— *(pretending to cry.)*

Mign. I'll tear you piece-meal, you villain, I
will.—

Wil. Don't break the peace woman—*(holds her.)*

Mign. I could cry my eyes out for vexation—
you impertinent jackanapes, to go for to talk to me
in this manner— *(crying.)*

Wil. Ay! now the fhower comes; let it wafh
her face;—well, your fervant, my dear,—adieu!

Mign. Yes, go your ways, do—

Wil. *(going, returns.)* You'll never fee us any
more.

Mign. So much the better.—

Wil. *(returning.)* We fhall never vifit you again.

Mign. Who defires your vifits?—

Wil. Not even if you fend for us.

Mign. Very well!—a good riddance—

Wil. Fare ye well!—you now fee the laft of me;
—and

—and harkye; don't break your heart;—adieu!—
don't let me find you hanging in the garret,—dang-
ling by an old wafh'd ribbon—do nothing rafhly—
time will cure your forrow—adieu.—*(Exit finging.)*

Mign. Ay, go thy ways for a vile, abandoned—
they fhall foon be expofed all over the town, that's
what they fhall; a couple of falfe, perfidious, vile
wretches.—*(Exit.)*

SCENE, Sir BASHFUL CONSTANT's.

Enter Lady CONSTANT *and* FURNISH.

Lady Con. Is the fervant waiting?

Fur. He is, Ma'am.

Lady Con. Very well; I need not write; give
my fervice to Mrs. Lovemore, and I fhall wait upon
her.

Fur. I fhall, Madam, *(going.)*

Lady Con. But, Furnifh;—have the things been
carried home to Sir Brilliant Fafhion, as I ordered?

Fur. They have, Madam.

Lady Con. Who went with them?

Fur. Your Ladyfhip's fteward; he is a trufty
body, and can be depended upon;—

Lady Con. Very well! Step and fend Mrs. Lovemore word, I fhall wait upon her.—*(Exit Furnifh.)*

Lady CONSTANT, *alone.*

Thofe diamond buckles muft certainly have been
fent to me by Sir Brilliant Fafhion; he has already
had the confidence to make difhonourable overtures
to me, and feeing what a hard card I have to play
with my hufband, he thinks, I fuppofe, to bribe
me to my ruin. Let me fee the letter I received with
them, *(reads)* " *Accept this prefent from one that*
" *adores you, and, whenever he fees you inclined to*
" *make a return to his affection, will declare himfelf*

I   " *farther*

" *farther to you.*"—It muft be Sir Brilliant ; no one elſe would preſume ſo far ;—however, I have treated him with the diſdain he merits.—But Mrs. Lovemore's card—what can be the meaning of it ? *(reads)* " *begs the favour of her Ladyſhip's company to cards* " *this evening.*"—Cards at Mrs. Lovemore's !—there is ſomething new in that—*(reads)* " *a particular af-* " *fair requires Mrs.* Lovemore's *friends to be pre-* " *ſent.*"—There is ſome myſtery in all this—what can it be ?—

Enter Sir BASHFUL.

Sir Bash. Here ſhe is ;—now let me ſee whether the preſent I have conveyed to her has put her into a better temper.—Your ſervant, Madam.—

Lady Con. Your ſervant, Sir.

Sir Bash. You ſeem out of humour, I think, Madam.

Lady Con. And, conſidering that you never give me cauſe—That is very ſtrange, is it not ?—

Sir Bash. My lady Conſtant, if you did not give me cauſe—

Lady Con. For heaven's-ſake, Sir, let us have no more diſagreeable altercation—I am tired of your violence of temper, your frequent ſtarts of paſſion ; your unaccountable fancies.

Sir Bash. Fancies, Madam ! do I only fancy that you are for ever making exorbitant demands upon me for the various articles of your expence ?—and when you are conſtantly teazing me for diamonds, and I know not what ; is that a fancy that I take into my head without foundation ?

Lady Con. Pray Sir, let us not diſpute—I promiſe never to trouble you on that head again—

Sir Bash. She is reſolved, I ſee, not to own that ſhe has received them—Stubborn, ſtubborn to the laſt, *(Aſide.)*

Lady

Lady Con. To be plain with you, Sir, I cannot any longer submit to be tormented with your humours—I have wrote to my sollicitor to attend us here to-morrow morning with the articles of sepation, and I presume, Sir, you will have no objection to their being finally executed.—I have no time to squander now in frivolous disputes—I must prepare to go out and pay a visit—your servant Sir— *(Exit.)*

Sir Bash. I must unburthen myself at last—must disclose the secrets of my heart; she has possessed my very soul; is ever present to my imagination; mingles with all my thoughts, inflames my tenderest passions, and raises such a conflict here—*(Striking his breast.)*—I cannot any longer keep this fire pent-up; I'll go, and throw myself open to her this moment—But then that chatter-box of a maid will be with her—I can turn her out of the room—but then she'll suspect something more than common—suppose I send to know whether she is alone!—Who's there?—Any body in the way?—

Enter SIDEBOARD.

Sir Bash. Step and see if any body is in the room?—What do you stand stock-still for?—Why don't you go?—

Side. What room does your honour mean?

Sir Bash. Can't you hear when you are spoken to?—Go and see if any body is in your lady's room?

Side. Now I understand you, Sir—what new whim has he taken into his head?—*(Going.)*

Sir Bash. And hark'e,—be sure you—No, no—It's no matter; it does not signify—you need not go at all.

Side. As you please, Sir—   *(Exit.)*

Sir Bash. *(Alone.)* Shall I venture or not?——That babbling minx of a maid, I can get rid off——But then, some of her visitors will be breaking in upon us—what can I do?—My friend Lovemore,

what

what keeps him away so long?—I can't risk the explanation myself—and yet—no—I had better drop it altogether—a thought comes across me———that's right—that will do—Ay, ay—'tis even so—I should never be able to go thro' it.—The glance of her eye, the warmth of my own desires,—my remorse,—my confusion—No, no,—it shall be the other way—Sideboard,—why don't you answer when I call?—

Enter SIDEBOARD.

SIDE. I came the very instant I heard you, Sir.

Sir BASH. Don't stand talking;—draw that table over this way—A letter will do the business—reach a chair—You blockhead, why don't you reach a chair?

SIDE. There, your Honour——

Sir BASH. Do you stay while I write a letter—You shall carry it for me—(*Sits down and writes.*)

SIDE. Yes, Sir—I hope he has got some intrigue upon his hands; a servant always thrives under a master that has his private amusements—Love on, say I, if you are so given; it will all bring grist to my mill—(*Aside.*)

Sir BASH. (*writing.*) Soft, passionate, and tender so far—and yet it does not come up to what I feel—it is a hard thing, in excessive love like mine, to speak as delicately as we think to the person we love—(*Aside.*)

SIDE. Let me see if there is any news in the paper to-day—(*Takes a paper out of his pocket and reads*)—Oh! Lord! Oh! Lord! I can't help laughing—Ha! ha!——

Sir BASH. (*stares at him.*) What does that rascal mean?—He does not suspect me, does he?—(*Stares at him, then rises.*) Hark'e Sirrah!—If ever I find that you dare listen at any door in my house, I'll cut your ears off, I will.

SIDE. Sir!——

Sir Bash. Confefs the truth;—Have not you been liftening to my converfation?

Side. Who I, Sir?—not I, Sir;—I never did the like in my born days.

Sir Bash. What was you laughing at, Rafcal?

Side. An article in the news-paper; that's all Sir—I'll read it to your Honour—(Reads.) We hear that a new comedy will fpeedily be acted, call'd " *The Amourous Husband, or the Man in Love with his own Wife.*"

Sir Bash. Well, and what do you fee to laugh at there?

Side. Lord blefs me Sir! I have lived in a great many families, and I never heard of the like before —Ha! ha!———

Sir Bash. Look'e there now!—Sirrah! leave the room—and let me never find that you have the trick of liftening at any of my doors.—

Side. No Sir—To be fure, your Honour—what is he at now? (*Exit.*)

Sir Bash. (*alone.*) Wounds! I fhall be laught at by my own fervants!—But no more fcruples,— pafs that by—I'll finifh my letter.—But then, if I fhould get into a comedy for my pains!—No, no; I'll run away into the country with her, to avoid the farcafms of the malicious world.—It fhall be fo, and fo I'll e'en conclude—There, there—I'll feal it up directly.—Sideboard, Sideboard.———

Enter SIDEBOARD.

Sir Bash. (*fealing the letter*) I have open'd my whole heart to her—why does not this fellow come? —Sideboard!

Side. Here am I, Sir?

Sir Bash. What do you take your hat and ftick for?

Side. To go out with your Honour's letter.

Sir Bash. You have not far to go—take it and
bring

bring me an anfwer—and do you hear ?—Take care
that nobody fees you—

SIDE. I warrant you, Sir. *(Exit.)*

Sir BASH. I feel as if a load was off my breaft ;
and yet I fear,—but I am embarked, and fo muft
wait the event.

Enter SIDEBOARD.

Sir BASH. Return'd already, Sideboard !—what,
is fhe not at home ?

SIDE. I can't fay, Sir ; a word or two by way of
direction will not be amifs—

Sir BASH. Blockhead ! have not I directed it ?
(Takes the Letter.)

SIDE. I could never have fufpected him of an intrigue. *(Afide.)*

Sir BASH. There again now !—If I direct it, this
hound will be upon the trail of a fecret—*(Afide.)*
—You may go about your bufinefs, Sideboard,
I don't want you—

SIDE. Very well, Sir ;—If he does not let me
manage his intrigues for him I fhall give him warn-
ing. *(Exit.)*

Sir BASH. What muft be done ?—Lovemore fhall
do it—Ha!——Sideboard coming again!——No ;
it is not he—Ha! Mr. Lovemore! I am glad to
fee you—

Enter LOVEMORE.

LOVE. You fee me here this fecond time to-day,
entirely on the fcore of friendfhip.—

Sir BASH. I thank you, Mr. Lovemore, heartily thank you—

LOVE. Well, and how does my lady ?

Sir BASH. We don't hit it at all, Mr. Lovemore—

LOVE. No !

Sir BASH. I think fhe has been rather worfe fince
you fpoke to her.

LOVE.

Love. A good fymptom that! *(Afide.)*

Sir Bash. Not a word of the buckles, tho' fhe has received them—obftinate as a mule!—She ftill talks of parting—and fo, to prevent extremities, I have even thought of explaining myfelf to her—

Love. What acquaint her with your paffion!

Sir Bash. Ay! and truft to her honour. I have wrote her a letter—here it is figned and fealed—but then it is not directed—I got into a puzzle about that; my fervant, you know, would wonder at my writing to her.

Love. So he would.

Sir Bash. Yes, he would have fmok'd me; but you are come moft opportune; you fhall direct, and fend it to her.

Love. I'll take it home with me, and fend it from my houfe to-morrow morning.

Sir Bash. No, no; now directly, now.

Love. You had better let me go and fpeak to her, and don't give any thing under your hand.

Sir Bash. That won't do; fhe'll fend a verbal anfwer; now, in this way, if I can draw a letter from her, I fhall have her bound down; it muft be fo—

Love. Better take a little time to confider of it—

Sir Bash. No, no; I can't defer it one moment; —Not one moment—it burns like a fire here—you muft be my friend—fit down; fit down and direct it,—

Enter SIDEBOARD.

Side. Sir Brilliant Fafhion, Sir, is below.

Love. 'Sdeath he muft not come up; run to him, talk to him, amufe him, any thing rather than let him interrupt us.

Sir Bash. No; he fhan't come up.

Love. You lofe time, away; and don't let him know

know that I am here—fly, Sir Bafhfull, fly—*(Shoves him out.)*

Love. *(alone.)* A lucky accident this! I have gained time by it.—Matters were in a fine train, and he himfelf levelling the road for me, and now, if this takes, I am blown up in the air at once.—Some unlucky planet rules to-day; firft the widow Bell-mour, and now this will-o'-the-wifp!—what in the name of wonder has he wrote? *(Going to open the Letter.)* But will that be delicate? will that be like a gentleman? will it be honourable?—Honour has always a great deal to preach on thefe occafions —But then muft I lofe the dear delight—Oh! the paffions need fay but a word, and their bufinefs is done. Friendfhip and wafer by your leave *(breaks it open and reads.)* this muft not be—I'll write ano-ther letter from myfelf—*(Sits down to write.)* What the devil fhall I fay?—Any thing will do—*(Writes and ftarts up as if frightened.)* There is no body coming *(writes and mutters to himfelf.)* Touched my heart—Hem! very well—Long adored,—very well! —Kind return,—very well!—Husband—very well! —Inhumanity, Hem! Tendernefs,—Hem!—Your fin-cereft admirer—very well!—Lovemore—what have I wrote?—let me fee—*(Reads faft.)* " *Why fhould*
" *I conceal, my dear Madam, that your charms have*
" *touched my heart? I long have loved you; long*
" *adored. Could I but flatter myfelf with the leaft*
" *kind return, I fhould be the happieft of mankind,*
" *let me perfuade you to the fweeteft revenge againft*
" *a husband, whofe inhumanity is beyond enduring.*
" *Every motive prompts you to it; and at the fame*
" *time you will enjoy the fecret pleafure of rewarding*
" *the tendernefs of your fincereft admirer,*"

Lovemore."

This will do! let me feal it—Soft! I muft add a poftfcript——*(writes, and then reads very faft.)*
" *You*

" *You need send no other answer but it's very well;*
" *and you'll consider of it.*"——There, there, make
haste, let me seal it up—(*Seals it in a hurry.*)

Enter SIR BASHFUL.

Sir BASH. Well! have you sent it?

LOVE. Your servant has not been here, and I am
just writing the direction—

Sir BASH. Who waits there? Sideboard!—I have
got rid of Sir Brilliant, Mr. Lovemore.

LOVE. I am glad of it.

Enter SIDEBOARD.

Sir BASH. Here, Sirrah! Mr. Lovemore, wants
you.

LOVE. Master Sideboard, you must step to your
lady with this.

Sir BASH. Charming! charming!—Take it up
stairs directly.

SIDE. Up-stairs Sir! My lady is in the next room.

Sir BASH. Take it to her then; make haste;
begone—(*Exit Sideboard.*) I hope this will succeed,
Mr. Lovemore.

LOVE. I hope it will.

Sir BASH. I shall for ever be obliged to you, and
so will my lady.

LOVE. I dare say she won't prove ungrateful.

Sir BASH. I should like to see how she receives
it;—the door is conveniently open; I'll have a
peep (*goes on tip-toe*) there,—there she sits.——

LOVE. Methinks I should like to observe her too.

Sir BASH. Hush!—No noise.—She has got it;
I am frightened out of my wits.

LOVE. Silence! not a word.—She opens it;—
Now, my dear boy Cupid, incline her heart. (*Aside.*)

Sir BASH. She colours!

LOVE. I like that rising blush—a tender token
that!—

Sir

Sir Bash. She turns pale!

Love. The natural working of the paffions.

Sir Bash. And now fhe reddens again!—Death and fury!—She tears the letter!—I am undone— *(Walks away from the door.)*

Love. She has flung it from her with indignation—I am undone too—*(Goes from the door.)*

Sir Bash. Mr. Lovemore, you fee what it is all come to!——

Love. I am forry to fee it come to this indeed.——

Sir Bash. An arrogant, ungrateful woman!—

Love. Ungrateful indeed!—To make fuch a return to fo kind a letter.

Sir Bash. Ay! fo kind a letter!—

Love. So full of the tendereft proteftations!—

Sir Bash. Made with the greateft opennefs of heart!—throwing ones-felf at her very feet; and then to be fpurned, kicked, and treated like a puppy.

Love. There it ftings—like a puppy indeed—

Sir Bash. Did fhe once fmile?—Was there the fainteft gleam of approbation in her countenance?

Love. Repaid it all with contempt, with fcorn, and indignation.—

Sir Bash. I cannot bear it;—My dear Mr. Lovemore, do you know in nature a thing fo mortifying, fo galling to the pride of man, as to find himfelf rejeéted and defpifed where he has offered up his heart?

Love. Oh! 'Tis the damndeft thing in the world—a fine fcrape I have got into here—*(Afide.)*

Sir Bash. Mr. Lovemore, I am heartily obliged to you, for taking this matter fo much to heart.

Love. I take it more to heart, than you are aware of, I affure you.—

Sir Bash. You are kind indeed; I am for ever obliged to you—This is enough to make a man afhamed all the reft of his life—

Enter

Enter SIR BRILLIANT.

Sir Bril. Sir Bashful! Sir Bashful! I forgot to tell you—Hey!—Lovemore here!

Sir Bash. What brings him here again?—those blockheads of servants to let him in—(*Aside.*)

Sir Bril. I have a crow to pluck with you, Lovemore.

Love. Well! well! another time. He hunts me up and down, as the vice did the devil, with a dagger of lath in the old comedy (*Aside.*)

Sir Bril. Upon my soul, you both look very queer upon it;—Lovemore is borrowing money of you, I suppose, Sir Bashful and you can't agree about the premium.—Come, come, let him have it —he is a very honest fellow—Still out of humour! —Well! as you will—You have not the same reason to be in harmony with yourselves, that I have. —Here, here;—I came back on purpose to tell you. —See here, my boys, what a present has been made me; (*Takes a shagreen case out of his pocket.*) a magnificent pair of diamond buckles, by Jupiter!

Sir Bash. A pair of diamond buckles!

Sir Bril. A pair of diamond buckles, Sir!—How such a thing should be sent to me I can't conceive; they were left at my house by a country-looking fellow; he would not say where he came from, but he left them in charge to be delivered to me.—The consequence of having some tolerable phrase,—a person—and being attentive to the service of the ladies.

Sir Bash. And this was sent as a present to you?

Sir Bril. Ay! as a present; do you envy me?

Sir Bash. I can't but say I do—My buckles, Lovemore, by all that's false in woman. (*Aside.*)

Love. He is the happy man, I see— (*Aside.*)

Sir Bril. Both burning with envy, by Jupiter!

Sir

Sir Bash. But may not this be from a lady; who imagines you fent them to her, and so chufes to reject your prefent?

Sir Bril. No, no;—No fuch thing—Ha! ha! —Ladies do not reject prefents, my dear Sir Bafhful, from men who are agreeable in their eyes.

Sir Bash. So I believe;—what a jade it is?
(Afide.)

Sir Bril. Had I fent them, they would 'never have been returned.

Sir Bash. And pray now, Sir Brilliant, I fuppofe you expect to have this lady?

Sir Bril. This is the fore-runner of it, I think—Ha! ha! Sir Bafhful—Lovemore!—this it is to be in luck.—Ha! ha! *(Laughs at them both.)*

Sir Bash.
Love. } Ha! ha! *(Both forcing a laugh.)*

Sir Bril. I fwear you are both ftrangely picqued —Lovemore, you feem uneafy.

Love. You wrong me, Sir—I—I—I am not uneafy.

Sir Bash. He frets on my account—Oh! he is a true friend. *(Afide.)*

Sir Bril. And, my dear Sir Bafhful, you repine at my fuccefs too.

Sir Bash. I can't but fay I do.

Sir Bril. Well you are not difpofed to be good company I fee—with all my heart—Lovemore, where do you fpend the evening?

Love. I can't fay Sir—I believe I fhall ftay here —Sir Bafhful and I are upon a little bufinefs.

Sir Bril. Are you?—very well—don't let me interrupt—finifh your money matters—adieu!— Your fervant, Gentlemen, your fervant—Thou dear pledge of love, *(Looking at the cafe)* let me clafp thee to my heart. *(Exit.)*

M   Sir

Sir BASHFULL and LOVEMORE.

Sir BASH. What think you now, Mr. Lovemore?

LOVE. All unaccountable, Sir.

Sir BASH. By all that's falfe, I am gulled, cheat-
ed, impofed upon, deceived and dubbed—I fuppofe fhe has given him my three hundred pounds
too.—I'll tell you what, if I can but get ocular
demonftration of her guilt,—if I can but prove to
the world that fhe is vile enough to cuckold me, I
fhall be happy.

LOVE. Why that will be fome confolation indeed!——

Sir BASH. So it will—Kind heaven! grant me
that—make it plain that fhe difhonours me—Hark!
Here her ladyfhip comes——

LOVE. 'Sdeath! let me fly the impending ftorm;
—Sir Bafhful, your humble fervant Sir. (Going.)

Sir BASH. You fhall not go; you fhall hear me
give her her own, and be a witnefs of our feparation.

LOVE. No; I can't bear the fight of her after
what has pafs'd; a good night Sir Bafhful; a good
night.

Sir BASH. (Standing between him and the door.) You
fhall ftay; I will not part with you.

Enter LADY CONSTANT.

Lady CON. I am furpriz'd, Mr. Lovemore, you
can think of ftaying a moment longer in this houfe.

LOVE. Madam!—How the devil fhall I give a
turn to this bufinefs? (Afide.)

Sir BASH. Mr. Lovemore is my friend, Madam,
and I defire he will ftay here as long as he likes,
Madam.

LOVE. All will come out, I fear. (Afide.)

Lady CON. Your friend, Sir Bafhful!—And do
you authorife your friend, to treat me in this manner?—I wonder, Mr. Lovemore, you would prefume

fume to fend me fuch a letter.—Do you come dif-guifed under a mafk of friendfhip—to undo me?

Sir BASH. A mafk of friendfhip!—I know him too well—and I defired him to fend that letter.

LOVE. Sir Bafhful defired me, Ma'am. *(Bow-ing refpectfully.)*

Sir BASH. I defired it, Madam; and there is not a word of truth in that letter.

LOVE. Not one word of truth, Ma'am.

Sir BASH. It was all done to try you, Madam.

LOVE. Merely to try you.

Sir BASH. By way of an experiment; juft to fee how you would behave upon it.

LOVE. Purely for an experiment.

Lady CON. And am I to be made your fport, Sir?—And could you, Mr. Lovemore, make your-yourfelf an accomplice in fo mean an attempt to en-fnare me?——

Sir BASH. To enfnare me!—She calls it enfnar-ing——

LOVE. He has pleaded for me moft admirably.

(Afide.)

Sir BASH. It is pretty plain that our tempers are not fitted to each other, and I am now ready to part when you pleafe, Madam;—Nay, I will part.

Lady CON. That is the only thing we can agree in, Sir.

Sir BASH. Had that letter come from another quarter, it would have been very acceptable, Ma-dam.

Lady CON. I difdain the imputation.

Sir BASH. Well! well!—I will vent no more re-proaches—this is the laft of our converfing together, and take this by the way; you are not to believe one word of that letter.

LOVE. Not one word of it to be believed, Ma'am.

Sir BASH. Mr. Lovemore knows it was a mere joke. And as to your being a fine woman, and as

to any paffion that any body has conceived for you,
—there was no fuch thing.—Was there Lovemore?

Love. Ha! he! He brings me off finely; thanks
to his wrong head. (*Afide.*)

Lady Con. Mighty well, gentlemen; aggravate
your ill ufage—

Sir Bash. It was all a bam, Madam;—all a bam;
—let us laugh at her, Lovemore—

Love. Silly devil! (*afide*)—ha! ha!

Sir Bash. All a bam; ha! ha!——

Lady Con. I cannot bear this any longer—is my
chair ready there?—you may depend, Sir, this is
the laft you will fee of me in your houfe.   (*Exit.*)

LOVEMORE *and Sir* BASHFUL.

Sir Bash. Agreed, Madam; agreed.——Lovemore, this was well managed.

Love. Charmingly!—I am forry I could not fucceed better.

Sir Bash. And fo am I.

Love. I have done my beft; and fo now I'll take
my leave, Sir Bafhful.

Sir Bash. You fhall not leave me in this diftrefs
—a little longer, Mr. Lovemore.

Love. Had your lady proved tractable, I fhould
not have cared how long I ftaid—but as things are
fituated,——your humble fervant, Sir——it's nine
o'clock; and I muft go home to my wife.

Sir Baih. Never let her know you love her.

Love. No, no!—

Sir Bash. You fee how it is.

Love. Ay! ay! well off this time, and Madam
Fortune, if I truft you again, you fhall play me
what prank you pleafe. (*Exit.*)

Sir Bash. Mr. Lovemore, a—good-night; but,
harkye, if I can ferve you with your lady.

Love.

Love. *(within.)* I thank you as much as if you had.

Sir Bash. Be sure you never own the letter.

Love. Depend upon it.

Sir BASHFUL *alone.*

No, no; never own it—Sideboard, light the gentleman out.—My lady Conftant! my lady Conftant! let me chafe her from my thoughts,—can I do it ?—rage, fury, love—no more of love—I am glad fhe has tore the letter however—odfo! yonder it lies in fragments on the ground; I'll pick it up directly, and never own a tittle of it. And as to Sir Brilliant, I fhall know how to proceed with Madam in regard to him—If I can once prove the fact, every body will fay I am very ill ufed by her. *(Exit.)*

End of the Fourth Act.

ACT V.

SCENE, an Apartment at Mr. LOVE-MORE's.

Enter Mrs. LOVEMORE elegantly drefs'd; MUS-LIN *following her.*

Muslin.

WHY to be fure, Ma'am, it is fo for certain, and you are very much in the right of it.

Mrs. Love. I fancy I am:—I fee the folly of my former conduct, and I am determin'd never to let my fpirits fink into a melancholy ftate again.

Mus. Why, that's the very thing, Ma'am, the very thing I have been always preaching up to you.
—Did

2

—Did not I always fay, fee company, Ma'am, take your fhare of pleafure, and never break your heart for any man. This is what I always faid.

Mrs. Love. It's very well, you need not fay any more now.

Mus. I always faid fo!—And what did the world fay? Heavens blefs her for a fweet woman! And a plague go with him for an inhuman, barbarous, bloody, murdering brute.

Mrs. Love. No more of thefe liberties, I defire.

Mus. Nay, don't be angry,—they did fay fo indeed.—But dear heart, how every body will be over-joy'd, when they find you have pluck'd up a little, —as for me, it gives me new life, to have fo much company in the houfe, and fuch a racketing at the door with coaches and chairs, enough to hurry a body out of one's wits.—Lard, this is another thing, and you look quite like another thing, Ma'am, and that drefs quite becomes you,—I fuppofe, Ma'am, you will never wear your negligée again. It is not fit for you indeed, Ma'am.—It might pafs very well with fome folks, Ma'am, but the like of you—

Mrs. Love. Prithee truce with your tongue, and fee who is coming up ftairs.

Enter Mrs. BELMOUR.

Mrs. Love. Mrs. Bellmour, I revive at the fight of you. Muflin do you ftep down ftairs, and do as I have ordered you.

Mus. What the duce can fhe be at now? *(Exit.)*

Mrs. Bell. You fee I am punctual to my time. —Well, I admire your drefs of all things.—Did you buy this filk on Ludgate-Hill?—It's mighty pretty.

Mrs. Love. I am glad you like it,—but under all this appearance of gaity, I have at the bottom but an aching heart.

Mrs.

Mrs. BELL. Be rul'd by me, and I'll anfwer for the event.—Why really, now you look juft as you fhou'd do.——Why fhou'd you negleft fo fine a figure?

Mrs. LOVE. You are fo civil, Mrs. Bellmour—

Mrs. BELL. And fo true too!—what was beautiful before, is now heightened by the additional ornaments of drefs; and if you will but animate and infpire the whole, by thofe graces of the mind, which I am fure you poffefs, the impreffion cannot fail of being effectual upon all beholders, and even upon the depraved mind of Mr. Lovemore.—You have not feen him fince—have you?

Mrs. LOVE. No,—not a glimpfe of him.

Mrs. BELL. I hope he has no other haunts—If he does but come home time enough, depend upon it my plot will take. Well, and have you got together a good deal of company?

Mrs. LOVE. Pretty well.

Mrs. BELL. That's right,—fhew him that you will confult your own pleafure.—Is Sir Brilliant of the party?

Mrs. LOVE. A-propos,—as foon as I came home I received a letter from him; my maid had taken it in.—He there preffes his addreffes with great warmth, begs to fee me again, and has fomething particular to tell me,—you fhall fee it.—Oh! lud, I have not it about me,—I left it in my dreffing-room, I believe; you fhall fee it by and by, I took your advice, and fent him word he might come;——that lure brought him hither immediately,——he makes no doubt of his fuccefs with me.

Mrs. BELL. Well! two fuch friends as Sir Brilliant and Mr. Lovemore, I believe, never exifted!

Mrs. LOVE. Their falfhood to each other is unparalleled.—I left Sir Brilliant at the whift-table, as foon as the rubber's out, he'll certainly quit his company

pany

pany in pursuit of me.—Apropos—My Lady Conftant is here—.

Mrs. Bell. Is fhe!

Mrs. Love. She is, and has been making the ftrangeft difcovery—Mr. Lovemore has had a defign there too!

Mrs. Bell. Is it poffible?—

Mrs. Love. Certainly fo—there is fufficient proof —you muft know, Ma'am, *(a rap at the door)* as I live and breath, I believe this is Mr. Lovemore.—

Mrs. Bell. If it is, every thing goes on fwimmingly within.

Mrs. Love. I hear his voice, it is he,—How my heart beats!

Mrs. Bell. Courage, and the day's our own.— Where muft I run?

Mrs. Love. In, there, Ma'am.—Make hafte,—I hear his ftep on the ftair-head.

Mrs. Bell. Succefs attend you,—I am gone.

(Exit.)

Mrs. Love. *(alone,)* I am frighten'd out of my fenfes,—what the event may be I fear to think,—but I muft go thro' with it.

Enter LOVEMORE.

Mrs. Love. Mr. Lovemore, you're welcome home.

Love. Mrs. Lovemore, your fervant. *(Without looking at her),*

Mrs. Love. It's fomewhat rare to fee you at home fo early.

Love. I faid I wou'd come home, did not I?— I always like to be as good as my word.—What cou'd fhe mean by this ufage? to make an appointment, and break it thus abruptly! *(Afide.)*

Mrs. Love. He feems to mufe upon it. *(Afide.)*

Love. I can't tell what to make of it,—fhe does not mean to do fo infamous a thing as to jilt me.

(Afide.)

(*Afide.*) Oh, Lord! I am wonderfully tir'd. (*Yawns, and finks into an arm'd chair.*)

Mrs. Love. You an't indifpos'd, I hope, my dear.

Love. No, my dear,—I thank you,—I am very well;—a little fatigu'd only, with jolting over the ftones all the way from the city.—I drank coffee with the old banker,—I have been there ever fince I went out this afternoon—Confoundedly tir'd.—Where's William?

Mrs. Love. Do you want any thing?

Love. Only my cap and flippers.—I am not in fpirits, I think. (*Yawns.*)

Mrs. Love. You never are in fpirits at home, Mr. Lovemore.

Love. I beg your pardon,—I never am any where more chearful, (*Stretching his arms.*) I wifh I may die, if I an't very happy at home,—very (*yawns*)—very happy!

Mrs. Love. I can hear otherwife.—I'm inform'd that Mr. Lovemore is the infpirer of mirth and good humour wherever he goes.

Love. Oh! you over-rate me; upon my foul you do.

Mrs. Love. I can hear, Sir, that no perfon's company is fo acceptable to the ladies; that 'tis your wit that infpirits every thing,—that you have your compliment for one, your fmile for another, a whifper for a third, and fo on, Sir,—you divide your favours, and are every where, but at home, all whim, vivacity, and fpirit.

Love. No,—no,—(*laughing,*) how can you talk fo?—I fwear, I can't help laughing at the fancy.—I all whim, vivacity, and fpirit! I fhall burft my fides.—How can you banter one fo?—I divide my favours too!—Oh, heavens! I can't ftand this raillery,—fuch a defcription of me!—I that am rather faturnine, of a ferious caft, and inclin'd to be pen-

N   five!

five! I can't help laughing at the oddity of the conceit.—Oh Lord! Oh Lord! *(Laughs.)*

Mrs. Love. Juſt as you pleaſe, Sir.—I ſee that I am ever to be treated with indifference. *(Walks acroſs the ſtage.)*

Love. *(riſes and walks the contrary way.)* I can't put this widow Bellmour out of my head. *(Aſide.)*

Mrs. Love. If I had done any thing to provoke this uſage,—this cold, inſolent contempt—*(walking.)*

Love. I ſhall never be at reſt 'till I know the bottom of it—I wiſh I had done with that buſineſs intirely ; but my deſires are kindled, and muſt be ſatiſfy'd *(Aſide.)*

(They walk for ſome time ſilently by each other.)

Mrs. Love. What part of my conduct gives you offence, Mr. Lovemore.

Love. Still harping upon that ungrateful ſtring !—but prithee don't ſet me a laughing again.—Offence !——nothing gives me offence, Child !——you know I am very fond—*(yawns and walks)*—I like you of all things, and think you a moſt admirable wife ;—prudent, managing,—careleſs of your own perſon, and very attentive to mine ;—not much addicted to pleaſure,—grave,—retir'd,—and domeſtic ;—govern your houſe——pay the tradeſmens bills, *(yawns)* ſcold the ſervants, and love your huſband : —upon my ſoul, a very good wife !—As good a ſort of a wife *(yawns)* as a body might wiſh to have. —Where's William ?—I muſt go to bed.—

Mrs. Love. To bed ſo early !—Had not you better join the company ?

Love. I ſhan't go out to night.

Mrs. Love. But I mean the company in the dining-room.

Love. What company ? *(Stares at her.)*

Mrs. Love. That I invited to a rout.

Love. A rout in my houſe !—and you dreſſed out too !—What is all this ?

Mrs.

Mrs. Love. You have no objection, I hope.—

Love. Objection! — no, — I like company, you know, of all things ;——I'll go and join them :—— Who are they all?

Mrs. Love. You know 'em all ;——and there's your friend Sir Brilliant there.

Love. Is he there?—I'm glad of it.—But pray now how comes this about?

Mrs. Love. I intend to do it often.

Love. Do ye?

Mrs. Love. Ay, and not look tamely on, while you revel luxurioufly in a courfe of pleafure ; I fhall purfue my own plan of diverfion.

Love. Do fo, do fo, Ma'am, the change in your temper will be very pleafing.

Mrs. Love. I fhall indeed, Sir,—I'm in earneft.

Love. By all means follow your own inclinations.

Mrs. Love. And fo I fhall, Sir, I affure ye.

(*Sings.*)

No more I pine,
Content is mine ;
That fhunfhine of the breaft !
The pangs of love
No more I prove ;
No cares difturb my reft.

Love. What the devil has come over her? and what in the name of wonder, does all this mean?

Mrs. Love. Mean Sir !—it means—it means— it means—how can you afk me what it means?— Well, to be fure, the fobriety of that queftion !— Do you think a woman of fpirit can have leifure to tell her meaning, when fhe is all air, alertnefs, plea- fure, and enjoyment?

Love. She's mad!—Stark mad!

Mrs. Love. You're miftaken, Sir, ——not mad, but in fpirits, that's all ;—no offence I hope.—Am I too flighty for you ?—perhaps I am,—you are of a

faturnine

saturnine difpofition, inclin'd to think a little, or fo.
—Well, don't let me interrupt you; don't let me
be of any inconvenience.—That would be the unpo-
liteſt thing—for a married couple to interfere and en-
croach on each other's pleaſures,——Oh hideous! it
would be gothic to the laſt degree. Ha! ha! ha! ·

Love. *(forcing a laugh.)* Ha! ha!—Ma'am, you,
ha! ha! you are perfectly right.

Mrs. Love. Nay, but I don't like that laugh
now,—I pofitively don't like it;—can't you laugh
out as you were us'd to do? for my part, I'm determined to do nothing elfe all the reſt of my life.

Love. This is the moſt aſtoniſhing thing! Ma'am,
I don't rightly comprehend—

Mrs. Love. Oh lud! oh lud!—with·that impor-
tant face.—Well, but come now, what don't you
comprehend?

Love. There is fomething in this treatment that
I don't fo well—

Mrs. Love. Oh! are you there, Sir!——How
quickly they, who have no fenfibility for the peace
and happineſs of others, can feel for themſelves, Mr.
Lovemore!—But that's a grave reflection, and I hate
reflection.

Love. What has ſhe got into her·head?—This
ſudden change, Mrs. Lovemore, let me tell you, is
a little alarming, and—

Mrs. Love. Nay, don't be frighten'd,—there is
no harm in innocent mirth, I hope; never look
fo grave upon it. —I aſſure ye, Sir, that though
on your part, you feem determin'd to offer conſtant
indignities to your wife,—and tho' the laws of reta-
liation wou'd in fome fort exculpate her, if, when
provok'd to the utmoſt.—exaſperated beyond all enduring, ſhe ſhould, in her turn, make him know
what it is to receive an injury in the tendereſt point—

Love. Madam! *(angrily.)*

Mrs. Love. Well, well, don't be frighten'd, I fay, I fhan't retaliate :—my own honour will fecure you there ;—you may depend upon it.—You won't come and play a game at cards ?—Well, do as you like ; —well,—you won't come? No, no, I fee you won't. —What fay you to a bit of fupper with us ?—Nor that neither ?——Follow your inclinations, it is not material where a body eats.—The company expects me ; your fervant Mr. Lovemore, yours, yours.

(Exit finging.)

Love. *(alone.)* This is a frolic I never faw her in before !—Laugh all the reft of my life!—Laws of retalion !—an injury in the tendereft point ;——the company expects me,——your fervant, my dear, yours, yours!—*(mimicking her)* What the devil is all this ?—Some of her female friends have been tampering with her.—Zouns !—I muft begin to look a little fharp after madam.—I'll go this moment into the card-room, and watch whom fhe whifpers with, whom fhe ogles with, and every circumftance that can lead to—*(going.)*

Enter MUSLIN *in a hurry.*

Mus. Madam, Madam,—here's your letter,—I wou'd not for all the world that my mafter—

Love. What, is fhe mad too? What's the matter, Woman ?

Mus. Nothing, Sir,—nothing,—I wanted a word with my lady, that's all, Sir.

Love. You wou'd not for the world that your mafter,—what was you going to fay ?—What paper's that ?

Mus. Paper, Sir !

Love. Paper Sir ! Let me fee it.

Mus. Lard, Sir !—how can you afk a body for fuch a thing. It's a letter to me, Sir,—a letter from the country,—a letter from my fifter, Sir,—fhe bids me to buy her a *Shiver de Fize* cap, and a fixteenth in the

the lottery ; and tells me of a number she dream't of, that's all, Sir,—I'll put it up.

Love. Let me look at it, give it me this moment? *(reads.)* To Mrs. Lovemore!—Brilliant Fashion. This is a letter from the country, is it?

Mus. That, Sir—that is—no Sir,—no ;—that's not sister's letter.—If you will give me that back, Sir, I'll shew you the right one.

Love. Where did you get this ?

Mus. Sir?

Love. Where did you get it ?—Tell me truth.

Mus. Deart heart, you fright a body so—in the parlour, Sir,—I found it there.

Love. Very well !—Leave the room.

Mus. The devil fetch it, I was never so out in my politicks, in all my days. *(Exit.)*

Love. *(alone.)* A pretty epistle truly this seems to be,—let me read it.

" Permit me, dear madam, to throw myself on my knees, (for on my knees I must address you) and in that humble posture, to implore your compassion." —*Compassion with a vengeance on him*—*(walks about)* " Think you see me now with tender, melting, supplicating eyes, languishing at your· feet :"—*Very well, Sir!*—" Can you find it in your heart to persist in cruelty ?—Grant me but access to you once more, and in addition to what I already said this morning, I will urge such motives" *urge motives, will ye ?*— " as will suggest to you, that you shou'd no longer hesitate in gratitude, to reward him, who still on his knees, here makes a vow to you of eternal constancy and love." BRILLIANT FASHION.

So ; so ! so!—your very humble servant, Sir Brilliant Fashion !—This is your friendship for me, is it ?—your mighty kind indeed, Sir,—but I thank you as much as if you had really done me the favour,——and, Mrs. Lovemore, I'm your humble servant too.—She intends to laugh all the rest of her
life !

life! This letter will change her note.—Odfo, yonder
fhe comes along the gallery, and Sir Brilliant in full
chafe of her.—They come this way,—cou'd I but
detect them both now!—I'll ftep afide, and who
knows but the devil may tempt 'em to their undoing,—at leaft I'll try,—a polite hufband I am——
There's the coaft clear for you, Madam.   (*Exit.*)

Enter Mrs. LOVEMORE, *Sir* BRILLIANT *after
her.*

Mrs. Love. I tell you, Sir Brilliant, your civility is odious,—your compliments fulfome,—and
your folicitations impertinent, Sir.——I muft make
ufe of harfh language, Sir,—you provoke me to it
and I can't refrain.

Sir Bril. By all my hopes we are now conveniently alone (*Afide.*) Not retiring to folitude and difcontent again, I hope, Madam!—Have a care, my
dear Mrs. Lovemore of a relapfe.

Mrs. Love. No danger of that, Sir, don't be fo
folicitous about me.—Why wou'd you leave the
company? let me intreat you to return, Sir.

Sir Bril. By heaven, there is more rapture in being one moment *vis-a-vis* with you, than in the
company of a whole drawing-room of beauties.——
Round you are melting pleafures, tender tranfports,
youthful loves, and blooming graces, all unfelt, neglected, and defpis'd, by a taftelefs, cold, languid,
unimpaffion'd hufband, while they might be all fo
much better employ'd to the purpofes of extacy and
blifs.

Mrs. Love. I am amaz'd, Sir, at this liberty,—
what action of my life has authoriz'd fuch bare-fac'd
affurance?——I defire, Sir, you will defift from this
unequall'd infolence. I am not to be treated in this
manner,—and, I affure you, Sir, that were I not
afraid of the ill confequences that might follow, I
                                        fhould

should not hesitate a moment to acquaint Mr. Lovemore with your whole behaviour.

Sir BRIL. She won't tell her husband then,——a
charming creature, and blessings on her for so con-
venient a hint,——she yields, by all that's wicked!——
What shall I say to overwhelm her senses in a flood
of nonesense? (*Aside.*)

Go my heart's envoys, tender sighs make haste,——
Still drink delicious poison from thy eye,——
Raptures and paradise
Pant on thy lip, and to thy heart be press'd.

(Forcing her all this time.)

Enter Mr. LOVEMORE.

LOVE. Zoons, this is too much.

Sir BRIL. What the devil's the matter now?
(*Kneels down to buckle his shoe.*) This confounded
buckle is always plaguing me.——My dear boy,
Lovemore,——I rejoice to see thee.

(*They stand looking at each other.*)

LOVE. And have you the confidence to look me
in the face?

Sir BRIL. I was telling your lady here, of the most
whimsical adventure—

LOVE. Don't add the meanness of falshood, to
the black attempt of invading your friend's happiness.——I did imagine, Sir, from the long intercourse
that has subsisted between us, that you might have
had delicacy enough, feeling enough, honour enough,
Sir,——not to meditate an injury like this.

Sir BRIL. Ay, ay, it's all over, I'm detected
(*Aside.*) Mr. Lovemore, if begging your pardon for
this rashness will any ways atone—

LOVE. No, Sir, nothing can atone. The provo-
cation you have given me, would justify my draw-
ing upon you this instant, did not that lady and this
roof protect you.

Sir BRIL. But, Mr. Lovemore.

LOVE.

Love. But, Sir——

Sir Bril. I only beg——

Love. Pray Sir,—Sir, I infift—I won't hear a word.

Sir Bril. I declare upon my honour——

Love. Honour! for fhame, Sir Brilliant, don't ufe the word.

Sir Bril. If begging pardon of that lady——

Love. That lady!—I defire you will never fpeak to that lady.

Sir Bril. Nay, but prithee, Lovemore—

Love. Po! Po! don't tell me, Sir—*(walks about in anger.)*

Enter Sir B A S H F U L.

Sir Bash. Did not I hear loud words among you? —I certainly did—What are ye quarrelling about?

Love. Read that, Sir Bafhful *(Gives him Sir Brilliant's Letter.)* Read that, and judge if I have not caufe—*(Sir Bafhful reads to himfelf.)*

Sir Bril. Hear but what I have to fay—

Love. No, Sir, no;—I have done with you for the prefent—as for you, Madam, I am fatisfied with your conduct—I was indeed a little alarmed, but, I have been a witnefs of your behaviour, and I am above harbouring low fufpicions—

Sir Bash. Upon my word Mr. Lovemore, this is carrying the jeft too far—

Love. Sir I—it is the bafeft thing, a gentleman can be guilty of—

Sir Bash. Why fo I think.—Sir Brilliant, *(To him afide.)* here take this letter, and read it to him—his own letter to my wife—*(Afide.)*

Sir Bril. Let me have it—*(Afide.)* *(Takes the letter.)*

Sir Bash. 'Tis indeed as you fay the worft thing a gentleman can be guilty of.

Love. 'Tis an unparallelled breach of friendfhip:

Sir Bril. Well, I can't fee any thing fo unparal-

O   lelled

lelled in it—I believe it will not be found to be without a precedent—as for example—(*Reads.*)

"To My Lady Conftant——

"*Why should I conceal, my dear Madam, that your charms have touched my heart?*"

LOVE. (*in amaze.*) Zoons! my letter—(*Aside.*) "*I long have lov'd you, long adored. Could I but flatter myself*"—(*Lovemore walks about uneasy; Sir Brilliant follows him.*)

Sir BASH. There, Mr. Lovemore, the bafeft thing a man can be guilty of!——

Sir BRIL. (*Reads*) "*Could I but flatter myself with the least kind return.*"——

LOVE. Confufion! Let me feize the letter out of his hand. (*Snatches it from him.*)

Sir BASH. The bafeft thing, a man can be guilty of, Mr. Lovemore!——

LOVE. All a forgery, Sir; all a forgery.

Sir BASH. That I deny; it's the very identical letter, my lady threw away with fuch indignation—My lady Conftant, how have I wrong'd you!—That was the caufe of your taking it fo much to heart, Mr. Lovemore, was it?——

LOVE. A mere contrivance to palliate his guilt.

Sir BRIL. Ha! ha! my dear Lovemore, I fuppofe you have been at this work with the widow Bellmour too.

LOVE. The widow Bellmour!—I never faw her but once in my life, and then it was to ferve you, Sir.——

Sir BRIL. Are you fure of that?

LOVE. Po! po! I won't ftay a moment longer among ye—I'll go into another room, to avoid ye all—I know little or nothing of the widow Bellmour, Sir, (*opens the ftage door.*) Hell and deftruction!—what fiend is conjured up here! Zoons! let me make my efcape out of the houfe (*Runs acrofs the ftage to the oppofite door*)——

Mrs. LOVE. I'll fecure this door—You muft not go, my dear.   LOVE.

Love. S'death, Madam, let me pafs.

Mrs. Love. Nay, you fhall ftay, I want to introduce an acquaintance of mine to you.

Love. I defire, Madam——

Enter Mrs. BELLMOUR.

Mrs. Bell. My Lord, my lord Etheridge; I
am heartily glad to fee your lordfhip (*Taking hold
of him.*)

Mrs. Love. Do, my dear, let me introduce this
lady to you (*Turning him to her.*)

Love. Here's the devil and all to do! (*Afide.*)

Mrs. Bell. My Lord, this is the moft fortunate
encounter——

Love. I wifh I was fifty miles off. (*Afide.*)

Mrs. Love. Mrs. Bellmour, give me leave to introduce Mr. Lovemore to you (*Turning him to her.*)

Mrs. Bell. No, my dear Ma'am, let me introduce lord Etheridge to you (*Pulling him.*) My
Lord——

Sir Bril. In the name of wonder, what is all this?

Sir Bash. Wounds! is this another of his intrigues blown up?

Mrs. Love. My dear Ma'am, you're miftaken;
this is my hufband.

Mrs. Bell. Pardon me, Ma'am, 'tis my lord
Etheridge.

Mrs. Love. My dear, how can you be fo ill-bred
in your own houfe?—Mrs. Bellmour,—this is Mr.
Lovemore.

Love. Are you going to tofs me in a blanket,
Madam?—call up the reft of your people, if you are.

Mrs. Bell. Pfhaw!—Prithee now, my Lord,
leave off your humours;—Mrs. Lovemore, this is
my lord Etheridge, a lover of mine, who has made
propofals of marriage to me.

Love. Confufion! let me get rid of thefe two
furies (*Breaks away from them.*)

Sir

Sir Bash. He has been tampering here too, has he?

Mrs. Bell. (*follows him,*)—My Lord I fay! my lord Etheridge!—won't your Lordſhip know me?

Love. This is the moſt damnable accident!

(*Aſide.*)

Mrs. Bell. I hope your Lordſhip has not forgot your appointment at my houſe this evening.

Love. Ay, now my turn is come. (*Aſide.*)

Mrs. Bell. Prithee, my Lord, what have I done, that you treat me with this coldneſs? Come, come, you ſhall have a wife, I will take compaſſion on you.

Love. Damnation! I can't ſtand this, (*Aſide.*)

Sir Bash. Murder will out—murder will out—

Mrs. Bell. Come, cheer up, my Lord;—What the duce, your dreſs is alter'd!—What's become of the ſtar and the ribband?—And ſo the gay, the florid, the magnifique lord Etheridge, dwindles down into plain Mr. Lovemore, the married man! Mr. Lovemore, your moſt obedient, very humble ſervant, Sir.

Love. I can't bear to feel myſelf in ſo ridiculous a circumſtance. (*Aſide.*)

Sir Bash. He has been paſſing himſelf for a lord; has he?—

Mrs. Bell. I beg my compliments to your friend Mrs. Loveit; and I am much oblig'd to you both for your very honourable deſigns—(*Curteſying to him.*)

Love. I never was ſo aſham'd in all my life!

Sir Bril. So, ſo, ſo, all his pains were to hide the ſtar from me.—This diſcovery is a perfect cordial to my dejected ſpirits.

Mrs. Bell. Mrs. Lovemore, I cannot ſufficiently acknowledge the providence, that directed you to pay me a viſit, tho' I was wholly unknown to you; and I ſhall henceforth conſider you as my deliverer.

Love.

Love. Zoons; It was fhe that fainted away in the clofet, and be damn'd to her jealoufy (*Afide*.)

Sir Bril. By all that's whimfical, an odd fort of an adventure this—My Lord, (*advances to him.*) my Lord,—my lord Etheridge, as the man fays in the play, " Your lordfhip's right welcome back to Denmark."

Love. Now he comes upon me.—Oh! I'm in a fine fituation. (*Afide.*)

Sir Bril. My Lord, I hope that ugly pain in your lordfhip's fide is abated.

Love. Abfurd, and ridiculous, (*Afide*)

Sir Bril. There is nothing forming there, I hope, my Lord.

Love. Damnation! I can't bear all this——Po! po!—No more, Sir Brilliant, don't tell me—(*goes toward the door in the back fcene.*) Here is another fiend—I am befet with them——

Enter Lady CONSTANT.

Love. No way for an efcape?—(*attempts both ftage doors, and is prevented.*)

Lady Con. Mr. Lovemore, it is the luckieft thing in the world, that you are come home—

Love. Ay, it's all over—Tell the fheriffs officers, I am ready—

Lady Con. I have loft every thing I play'd for; quite broke; four by honours againft me, every time—Do Mr. Lovemore, lend me another hundred.

Love. I would give a hundred pound you were all in *Nova Scotia*.

Lady Con. Nay, then take the reft of your mo-ney; I will have nothing to do with it——

Sir Bash. Zookers, that money—Oh! I am going to blab—

Lady

Lady Con. There, Sir, I defpife it and the intention with which it was offered—(*Throws the notes to him.*)

Love. (*picking them up.*) This will plague Sir Bafhful however (*Afide.*)

Lady Con. Mrs. Lovemore, let me tell you, you are married to the falfeft man; he has deceived me ftrangely.

Mrs. Love. I begin to feel for him, and to pity his uneafinefs.

Mrs. Bell. Never talk of pity; let him be probed to the quick.

Sir Bash. The cafe is pretty plain, I think now, Sir Brilliant.

Sir Bril. Pretty plain, upon my foul—Ha! ha!

Love. I'll turn the tables upon Sir Bafhful, for all this—(*Takes Sir Bafhful's letter, out of his pocket.*) where is the mighty harm now, in this letter?

Sir Bash. Where is the harm?——

Love. (*Reads.*) " I cannot, my deareft life, any " longer behold——

Sir Bash. Shame and confufion! I am undone.
(*Afide.*)

Love. Hear this, Sir Bafhful—" *The manifold* " *vexations, of which thro' a falfe prejudice I am my-* " *felf the occafion.*

Lady Con. What is all this?

Sir Bash. I am a loft man (*Afide.*)

Love. Mind, Sir Bafhful. " *I am therefore re-* " *folved, after many conflicts with myfelf, to throw off* " *the mafk, and frankly own a paffion, which the fear of* " *falling into ridicule has in appearance fuppreffed.*"

Sir Bash. 'Sdeath! I'll hear no more of it——(*Snatches at the letter.*)

Love. No, Sir; I refign it here, where it was directed, and with it, my lady Conftant, thefe notes which Sir Bafhful gave me for your ufe.

Lady

Lady Con. This is all a myſtery!—it is his hand ſure enough—

Love. Yes, Madam, and thoſe are his ſentiments, which he explained to me more at large.

Lady Con. (reads.) " *Accept the preſents which* " *I myſelf have ſent you ; money, attendance, equipage,* " *and every thing elſe you ſhall command ; and in re-* " *turn, I ſhall only entreat you to conceal from the* " *world that you have raiſed a flame in this heart,* " *which will ever ſhew me,*

" *My deareſt life,*

" *Your moſt affectionate huſband,*

" Bashful Constant.

All. Ha! ha!—

Sir Bril. So, ſo, ſo!—he has been in love with his wife all this time, has he?—Sir Baſhful, will you go and ſee the new comedy with me?—

Sir Bash. I ſhall bluſh thro' the world all the reſt of my life *(Aſide.)*

Sir Bril. But, Lovemore, this is a pretty come-off—Pray now, don't you think it a baſe thing to invade the happineſs of a friend? or to do him a clandeſtine wrong? or to injure him with the woman he loves?—

Love. To cut the matter ſhort with you, Sir,—we are both raſcals.

Sir Bril. Raſcals!

Love. Ay! both! we are pretty fellows indeed!—

Mrs Bell. I am glad to find you are awakened to a ſenſe of your error.

Love. I am, Madam, and I am frank enough to own it—I am above attempting to diſguiſe my feelings, when I am conſcious they are on the ſide of truth and honour,—and, Madam, with a ſincere re-morſe,

morſe, I aſk your pardon.—I ſhould aſk pardon of
my lady Conſtant too, but the truth is, Sir Baſhful
threw the whole affair in my way; and, when a
huſband will be aſhamed of loving a valuable woman, he muſt not be ſurpriſed if other people take
her caſe into conſideration, and love her for him.—

Sir Bril. Why, faith that does in ſome ſort apologize for him—

Sir Bash. Sir Baſhful! Sir Baſhful! thou ar't
ruin'd—(*Aſide.*)

Mrs. Bell. Well, Sir, upon certain terms, I
don't know but I may ſign and ſeal your pardon—

Love. Terms!—what terms!——

Mrs. Bell. That you make due expiation of
your guilt to that lady.

Love. That lady, Ma'am!—That lady has no
reaſon to complain.

Mrs. Love. No reaſon to complain, Mr. Lovemore!

Love. No, Madam,—none! for whatever may
have been my imprudences, they have had their
ſource in your conduct.

Mrs. Love. In my conduct, Sir!

Love. In your conduct!—I here declare before
this company,—and I am above palliating the matter, I here declare, that no man in England cou'd
be better inclin'd to domeſtic happineſs, if you, Madam, on your part, had been willing to make home
agreeable.

Mrs. Love. There I confeſs he touches me.

(*Aſide.*)

Love. You cou'd take pains enough before marriage,—you would put forth all your charms,—prac-
tiſe all your arts,—and make your features pleaſe
by rule;—for ever changing,—running an eternal
round of variety:—and all this to win my affections:—but when you had won them, you did not
think them worth your keeping ——Never dreſs'd,
pen-

penfive,—filent,—melancholy;—and the only en-
tertainment in my houfe, was the dear pleafure of a
dull conjugal *Tete-a-Tete*; and all this infipidity,
becaufe you think the fole merit of a wife confifts
in her virtue:—a fine way of amufing a hufband,
truly!

Sir Bril. Upon my foul, and fo it is—*(Laughing.)*

Mrs. Love. Sir, I muft own there is too much
truth in what you fay — this lady has open'd my
eyes, and convinc'd me there was a miftake in my
former conduct.

Love. Come, come, you need fay no more.—I
forgive you—I forgive—

Mrs. Love. Forgive!—I like that air of confidence, when you know that on my fide, it is at
worft an error in judgment, whereas on yours—

Mrs. Bell. Po! Po! never ftand difputing—
you know each others faults and virtues—you have
nothing to do but to mend the former, and enjoy
the latter—There, there, there,—kifs and be friends
—There, Mrs. Lovemore, take your reclaim'd libertine to your arms.—

Love. 'Tis in your power, Madam, to make a
reclaim'd libertine of me indeed.

Mrs. Love. From this moment it fhall be our
mutual ftudy to pleafe each other—

Love. A match with all my heart—I fhall here-
after be afhamed only of my follies, but never fhall
be afhamed of owning that I fincerely love you—

Sir Bash. Shan't you be afham'd?

Love. Never Sir—

Sir Bash. And will you keep me in countenance
then?

Love. I will.

Sir Bash. Give me your hand—I forgive you all
from the bottom of my heart—My Lady Conftant,

P   I own

I own the letter, I own the fentiments of it, *(em-braces her)* and from this moment I take you to my heart.

Lady Con. If you hold in this humour, Sir Bafh-ful, our quarrels are at an end.

Sir Bril. And now is my turn to make reftitu-tion here—— *(Gives lady Conftant the buckles.)*

Sir Bash. Ay, ay, make reftitution—Lovemore! This is the confequence of his having fome tolerable phrafe—and a perfon, Mr. Lovemore! ha! ha!——

Sir Bril. Why, I own the laugh is againft me; with all my heart; for faith, I am glad to fee my friends happy at laft—Lovemore, may I prefume to hope for pardon at that lady's hands *(points to Mrs. Lovemore.)*

Love. My dear confederate in vice, your par-don is granted.—Two fad dogs we have been,—but come, give us your hand,—we have us'd each other damnably—for the future we will endeavour to make each other amends.

Sir Bril. And fo we will.

Love. And now I heartily congratulate the whole company, that this bufinefs has had fo happy a ten-dency to convince each of us of our folly.

Mrs. Bell. Pray, Sir, don't draw me into fhare of your folly.

Love. Come, come, my dear Ma'am, you are not without your fhare of it. This will teach you for the future, to be content with one lover at a time, without liftening to a fellow you know nothing of,—becaufe he affumes a title, and reports well of himfelf.

Mrs. Bell. The reproof is juft, I grant it.

Love. Come, let us join the company chearfully, keep our own fecrets, and not make ourfelves a town-talk.——

Sir Bash. Ay, ay; let us keep the fecret.

Love. What, returning to your fears again?

3   Sir

Sir Bash. I have done.——

Love. Tho' faith, if this bufinefs were known in the world, it might prove a very ufeful leffon. The men would fee how their paffions may carry them into the danger of wounding the bofom of a friend, ——the ladies wou'd learn, that after the marriage rites, they fhou'd not fuffer their powers of pleafing to languifh away, but fhou'd ftill remember to facrifice to the graces.

To win a man, when all your pains fucceed,
The Way to Keep Him, *is a tafk indeed.*

F I N I S.

SONG for Mrs. CIBBER in the WAY TO KEEP HIM. Third Act.

Words by Mr. GARRICK. Musick by Dr. ARNE.

I.

*Y*E fair married dames who so often deplore,
   That a lover once bless'd, is a lover no more;
Attend to my counsel, nor blush to be taught,
That prudence must cherish, what beauty has caught.

II.

The bloom of your cheek, and the glance of your eye,
Your roses and lilies may make the men sigh:
But roses, and lilies, and sighs pass away,
And passion will die, as your beauties decay.

III.

Use the man that you wed, like your fav'rite GUITTAR,
Tho' music in both, they are both apt to jar;
How tuneful and soft from a delicate touch,
Not handled too roughly, nor play'd on too much.

IV.

The SPARROW *and* LINNET *will feed from your hand;*
Grow tame by your kindness, and come at command;
Exert with your husband the same happy skill,
For hearts, like your birds, may be tam'd to your will.

V.

Be gay and good-humour'd, complying and kind,
Turn the chief of your care from your face to your
     mind;
'Tis there that a wife may her conquests improve,
And HYMEN *shall rivet the fetters of* LOVE.